THE YEAR THE WOLVES CAME

BEBE FAAS RICE

The Year the Wolves Came

DUTTON CHILDREN'S BOOKS

New York

Library of Congress Cataloging-in-Publication Data
Rice, Bebe Faas. The year the wolves came /
by Bebe Faas Rice.—1st ed. p. cm.
Summary: Fourteen-year-old Therese recalls life on her
family's farm on the Canadian prairie during the winter
of 1906 when the arrival of both blizzards and wolves
leads to a terrifying revelation about her beautiful,
other-worldly mother. ISBN 0-525-45209-5
[1. Werewolves—Fiction.] I. Title. PZ7.R3615Ye 1994
[Fic]—dc20 94-20460 CIP AC

Published in the United States
by Dutton Children's Books,
a division of Penguin Books USA Inc.
375 Hudson Street, New York, New York 10014
Designed by Adrian Leichter
Printed in U.S.A.
First Edition
1 3 5 7 9 10 8 6 4 2

To my mother, her sisters,
and their parents,
who homesteaded in Canada
when wolves haunted the prairie . . .

CONTENTS

THE YEAR THE WOLVES CAME

▪ Chicago—1910 ▪

I've been having nightmares lately.

They are always the same, and they bring the same memories with them—cold fragments of memories, like bits and pieces of dismembered corpses. Memories I have tried desperately to bury.

I dream of torches flaring against a cold winter sky, with the stars so clear and white you can almost reach up and touch them. The moon is large and full. There is something frightening about that moon.

And there is always snow—white, glittering snow. Snow, and the sound of people shouting. And Papa, trembling, as he thrusts my little brother Joey and me up the steps of the train.

The train. That awful, terrible train. It crouches there, panting. Like a wounded animal. Like . . . like a wolf.

And then I see Mama. She is wearing a long, white nightgown, and there is something . . . a splash of something red . . . all down the front.

She stretches out her arms to me as if asking for help. Her eyes, her beautiful, silvery grey eyes plead with me. But there is nothing I can do.

It's too late.

It's too late because already I can hear the howling of the wolves, and they are coming closer. . . .

We are older now, Joey and I. Four years older than we were when the Terrible Thing happened. A short time for me, because I remember. A long time for Joey, who does not.

We live with Papa in a big brownstone apartment in Chicago. We are happy enough, I suppose. Papa has a good job, and Joey and I go to a fine new school.

Our apartment is very nice. We have a sink in

the kitchen with water that runs from faucets—
hot from one, cold from the other. No more haul-
ing water from an outside pump and heating it on
the big woodstove, as we did on the farm. And
there is even an inside bathroom, all tiled in blue,
with a bathtub and a little mirrored cabinet over
the hand basin. Mama would have enjoyed all this
luxury. Mama always loved pretty things.

We have a different last name now, too. Papa
went to a lawyer and had our old one changed.
When I asked him why, Papa only would say that
he liked the new one better.

I think I know the real reason, though. He's
afraid that someone someday might recognize our
old name and ask us about that last winter in
Canada. And then, of course, they might start
asking questions about Mama. Mama was so
lovely, so . . . different. People were always fascinated by her.

Dear, beautiful Mama. How I miss her.

I can still see her pale, silvery gilt hair, braided
and twisted in a thick crown around her head,
framing the delicate white oval of her face. And

I see her eyes—those large, slanting, grey eyes. Kind eyes. Loving eyes.

Papa is still a young man, for a father, but he looks old now. When we left Canada, his hair turned grey almost overnight. And recently he has begun to walk with a stoop, just like Mr. Schmidt, our new iceman.

Papa doesn't smile very often anymore. When he does, it's only with his lips. The corners of his mouth turn up, but his eyes remain bleak and tired-looking.

Sometimes in the evenings, when he thinks Joey and I are busy with our homework, he sits in the kitchen, his elbows on the table and his hands over his face.

Poor Papa! I hate it when he does that, because I know he is thinking of Mama.

Joey was only five when the Terrible Thing happened.

He was too young at the time to realize what was happening, or to remember clearly that last winter in Canada. And he seldom talks about Mama, rarely asks questions about her. Maybe, young as he is, he senses the something that is better left unsaid—something secret and forbidden.

Papa thinks Joey has forgotten Mama, but I know otherwise.

On cold winter nights, when the wind from the lake whistles beneath our bedroom window, I hear Joey call out in his sleep.

"Mama! Mama!"

I go over to him and sit on the bed beside him. I take his small, cold hand and pat it, the way Mama did when I was little and frightened.

"Joey! Wake up, Joey! You're having a bad dream."

"Oh, Therese . . . ," says Joey, opening his eyes slowly. His eyes, brown and long-lashed, are just like Papa's. But now they are worried-looking. He clings to my hand. "Mama was very beautiful, wasn't she? And she loved us. Didn't she love us?"

"Yes, Joey, she was very beautiful," I answer. "And she loved us very much. Don't you remember?"

Joey thinks a minute, then smiles, remembering, and falls asleep again.

I gently cover him with his eiderdown quilt and sit looking down on his round little face until I'm sure he won't awaken again.

Then I tiptoe back to my bed and snuggle down, trying to get warm again, and I think of how it was when we lived on the prairie, cozy and happy, when Papa had dark hair and smiled with his eyes.

I remember how much we all loved Mama. How kind and gentle she was.

And then I lie there in the dark, my head spinning, remembering how our world went crazy and upside down that strange, terrible winter when the wolves came.

ONE

Canada—1906

I was just ten years old that winter, the year the wolves came.

We had our first snowfall of the season on my birthday. It was a thin, light fall and lay on the ground clean and fresh and sparkling, like the white sugar frosting on the cake Mama baked and decorated with pink candles.

My birthday was always extra-special because my mother celebrated hers on that day, too. We had twice as many presents, two singings of the happy birthday song, and twice as much happiness.

I never could get over my good luck in being born on Mama's birthday. Since I wanted to be exactly like her when I grew up, I figured sharing a birthday with her was a good start.

I always thought my mother looked like a princess from a book of fairy tales, one of those illustrated with fragile, flowing pen drawings. She was gentle and quiet, too, the way princesses are supposed to be. I used to think that if I put a pea under her mattress at night, she would wake up bruised and sore in the morning. At local gatherings—quilting bees and barn raisings—when Mama moved smiling and gracious among all the sun-browned, bustling farmers' wives, she looked as delicate and out of place as visiting royalty.

Not many ten-year-old girls love their mothers the way I did mine, but then no one has ever had a mother like Mama.

But a few days after my tenth birthday, I found out the real reason why Mama celebrated her birthday with mine. Neither Mama nor Papa told me. I had to find it out from old Mrs. Kopek.

Mrs. Kopek was our closest neighbor. Her

weather-beaten frame house lay a short distance from ours, across the narrow end of her west pasture. I used to visit her often.

Papa said Mrs. Kopek was a busybody—a gossip. But Mama, who always thought the best of everyone, said Mrs. Kopek liked to talk because she was lonely. Mr. Kopek had died a few years back, and their sons had since married and moved away.

"The dear old lady needs someone to talk to," Mama would say. "It's very neighborly of you, Therese, to visit her as often as you do."

Mrs. Kopek always wore black, widow's black, to show proper grief for the death of her husband. Her dresses all looked alike to me—high-necked and buttoned down the front, with long, tight sleeves. I think she made them from the same pattern.

She must have been quite beautiful when she was young, because she was still a striking woman. She had lovely, high cheekbones and a delicately arched nose, and her eyes were a bright periwinkle blue. Her hair, although snow white, was still thick and wavy. She wore it pulled up and piled high on her head with little curls across her forehead.

"That's the way Mr. Kopek liked it," she told me once, "so that's how I've always worn it."

When I visited Mrs. Kopek's house, she treated me like an honored guest—like a grown-up. She'd make tea for us and serve it in her best bone-china cups, with a pile of freshly baked cookies carefully arranged on a blue-and-white plate.

And then she'd begin to talk!

If Mama had known what Mrs. Kopek was telling me, she probably would have forbidden my visits. She would have said I was too young to learn the dark, unhappy circumstances that led to Mrs. Kessler's suicide. Or how Mr. Povich desperately wanted a son and was angry with his wife for failing to produce one. Or all the exciting details of the Holmberg girl's recent elopement with the traveling salesman.

Sometimes Mrs. Kopek would get up from her chair and act out the story she was telling. She was a natural-born storyteller and could mimic just about anyone. When she scowled and spoke in a harsh, raspy voice, she sounded exactly like Mr. Povich. And when she fluttered her eyelashes and threw back her head, I could almost *see* that boy-crazy Holmberg girl!

I don't know why she decided to tell me about Mama that day. Maybe she thought I was finally old enough to know the truth. Or maybe her storytelling nature got the best of her—that it was such a strange, wonderful tale she simply had to tell it. In any case, I'm sure she meant no harm.

"But Therese," she said, "your Mama doesn't know when her real birthday *is*! Hasn't she ever told you that she knows nothing about her past?"

"No," I mumbled through a mouthful of cookies. As far as I was concerned, Mama's past began when I was born.

Mrs. Kopek sighed and leaned back in her chair. Her teacup made a musical little *clink* when she set it on the saucer. Her blue eyes took on a faraway expression.

"It was like a fairy tale," she said. "One of those old Russian ones my grandmother used to tell."

"A fairy tale? Oh, tell it to me, please!" I begged.

Maybe now I'd find out what I'd always suspected—that Mama really *was* a princess. Of course. That explained everything!

"It was a cold, cold winter," Mrs. Kopek began. "Your Papa had come up from Minnesota to homestead here in Canada. He was living with us until the weather grew warmer and he could build his house."

I nodded quickly. I already knew that part of the story. Papa, the youngest in a family of boys, had prospects of only a small inheritance. So he left the family farm and came north to Canada, lured by the promise of free land—a homestead of 160 acres. All Papa had to do was file papers for it and farm the land.

"And it was cold?" I prompted.

"Oh, it was terrible," said Mrs. Kopek. "We had one blizzard after another. Food began to run short because we couldn't get into town for supplies, not that there was much to be had even there, since the trains from Regina weren't running. Nothing but blowing winds and snow, day after day. The wolves had come down from the north, too, hungry and looking for game."

She paused, remembering.

I shuddered, imagining those wolves and their big, sharp teeth.

"The way they howled at night . . ." She made the sign of the cross on her breast. "They sounded like lost souls, crying to God. It made my blood run cold, just to hear them."

"Did they . . . *do* anything?"

"They seemed to keep their distance, staying on the far side of the prairie. Maybe they found some snowshoe rabbits or some other winter game out there. But we kept our barns locked and barred tightly, just in case they'd try to get at the livestock. And of course, no one rode out at night for any reason."

"But where was Mama?" I asked.

She held up her hand and frowned. "I'm coming to that, Therese. All will be told, in due time."

It was useless to hurry Mrs. Kopek when she was telling a story. I ought to know that by now,

I told myself. So I took another bite of cookie, another sip of tea, and waited.

Mrs. Kopek refilled her cup, blew on the tea to cool it, and set it down carefully, placing her spoon on the saucer and lining it up parallel with the handle of the cup.

Then she leaned forward across the table toward me. Her face was now level with mine.

"One night," she began, her voice dropping even lower, "one bitterly cold night, the three of us—Mr. Kopek, your Papa, and I—were sitting around the stove, trying to keep warm. The wind was so strong! It seemed to whistle right through the walls of the house, although they were plastered snugly."

I put down the cookie I was holding and sat perfectly still.

"I was winding wool that night. Mr. Kopek was reading, and I think your Papa was mending a harness, trying to keep busy.

"And then our dog, Baron, who was normally friendly and gentle, stood up and growled. The hairs on his neck stuck straight up! It was the strangest thing. I'd never seen him in such a state, and he'd been with us for nearly ten years.

"He stood there, his head down, his lips pulled back from his teeth, making a rumbling sound in his throat. He seemed to be listening to something. Then, suddenly, he flung himself at the kitchen door, howling and carrying on as if he'd been possessed by the very devil himself. 'What is it?' I asked Mr. Kopek, may his dear soul rest in peace. 'Someone—or something—is out there,' he answered."

"What?" I whispered. "What was out there? Was it a wolf?"

Mrs. Kopek continued as though I hadn't interrupted.

"Your Papa reached the door first and pulled it open. He had to fight the wind to do so. And there, on the doorstep, lay a woman dressed all in white. A beautiful, snow princess of a woman."

I was barely breathing now. "Was it Mama? The woman . . . was it . . . she . . . Mama?"

"Yes, darling, it was your Mama."

Mrs. Kopek raised her right hand up, as if taking a vow. "Every word I'm saying is the God's truth. That is exactly how it happened. She'd come to us through that terrible storm and lay there, like a phantom, on our doorstep.

"We had to shut Baron in the storeroom. We were afraid he might attack her, he was still so crazy and excited. Then your Papa carried your mother over to the fire. She was nearly frozen. At first we thought she was dead. But finally she opened her eyes, those lovely, grey eyes. . . ."

"Did she say anything?"

"Yes. She asked where she was."

"She didn't know where she was?"

"No. And she had no idea *who* she was, either. Or how she had managed to find our house in the blizzard. She told us the only thing she could remember was that she had been running and running."

"But she had to come from somewhere!" I insisted.

"That's what we thought, of course," Mrs. Kopek replied. "We took her upstairs to the spare bedroom and put her to bed. I wrapped her in heated flannels with a hot water bottle at her feet and covered her with eiderdown quilts. Then I began to spoon hot broth and tea into her. But even when she'd warmed up, she still couldn't remember anything about herself."

"Nothing? Nothing at all?"

Mrs. Kopek shook her head. "Nothing. And to this very day, she can't remember her past."

I must have had an expression of disbelief on my face because Mrs. Kopek said quickly, "Have you ever heard her speak of when she was growing up? No? Well then, you see!

"Your Papa was nearly wild to find out who she was and if she had a husband. He'd fallen desperately in love with her, you see, the very first moment he laid eyes on her. I've never seen a man so crazy in love."

Papa is still crazy in love with Mama, I thought. I can tell.

"So what happened next?" I asked.

"When the weather warmed, your Papa rode to all the neighboring towns and asked if they were searching for a missing woman."

"Were they?"

"No. No one seemed to know anything about her. It was as though she'd appeared out of nowhere, just like in a fairy tale. Strange, wonderful things like that still happen, you know, even in these times."

I couldn't reply. I sat there, chewing over Mrs. Kopek's words. Strange, she had said. Wonderful. And fairy tale. Of course. Those words described my feelings about Mama perfectly.

"And that's how we must think of it, Therese. We will never know where your mother came from and what she was doing out there in the blizzard that night. She simply cannot remember, and to ask her about it only distresses her. But it all worked out well, didn't it?"

I knew the rest of the story, what happened next, but Mrs. Kopek told it to me anyway.

"And so your Papa married your Mama, and first you were born, then Joey. And now here you all are, living happily ever after."

A slight frown creased her forehead. "But . . ."

"But what?" I asked.

"The one thing I still can't understand is why your Mama was running through the snow in her bare feet."

"Her bare feet? She wasn't wearing any shoes?"

"No. Her poor little feet were cut and bleeding and nearly frozen. I don't know why she wasn't wearing shoes."

·The·Blizzard·

I didn't tell my parents what I learned that day.
I was afraid they wouldn't let me go to Mrs. Kopek's house anymore if they found out she was telling me things I wasn't supposed to know. But,
more than that, I didn't want to upset Mama or
make her sad by asking her about what had happened all those years ago.

Besides, we were all so busy getting ready for
the blizzards Pinky said were coming that I didn't
have a chance to think about it much.

Pinky was our hired man. He worked on the

farm and lived in the bunkhouse, out beyond the barn.

We all loved Pinky. That wasn't his real name, of course. Everyone called him that because of his coloring. His skin, hair, and eyelashes were white, but his lips were very pink. Even his eyes, a pale, pale blue, were rimmed with pink. Papa said Pinky was what was known as an albino.

When Pinky first came to work at the farm, Papa didn't want to call him by that nickname. He was afraid it was rude. But Pinky only laughed and said it was easier to pronounce than his real name, which was long and foreign.

Pinky had come to Canada from Russia. That's why he knew so much about blizzards. He said they had a lot of blizzards in Russia.

He also said they had a lot of wolves in Russia. Pinky knew all about wolves.

Anyway, Pinky had been telling us for weeks it would be a long, harsh winter.

"The geese flew south earlier this year than they usually do," he told us. "The crows have flown south, too, and all the game animals have disappeared. Even the jackrabbits have gone into hiding. And look at the thick coats on the livestock. They are preparing for the worst."

Joey and I were excited at the thought of blizzards and being snowbound for days and days! It would be something new for Joey. Well, maybe not new, exactly. We'd had a really bad winter a couple of years earlier, but he'd been too little at the time to remember.

I remembered, though. I thought those snowstorms were wonderful because I got to stay home from school.

Our community of homesteaders had banded together a few years before and built a little one-room schoolhouse. It sat out in the middle of the farmlands, on a half acre of unplowed prairie, where an old buffalo path intersected with what used to be an Indian trail.

There weren't any buffaloes left on the prairie now. They'd all been killed by hide hunters. But every now and then a farmer would turn up the bones of one, and sometimes, if it was really old, there'd be an arrowhead in it.

The Indians were gone from our part of the

country, too, just like the buffaloes they once hunted. And so, where hunter and hunted had met, there now stood a little white one-room schoolhouse.

Our teacher was an Englishman. Although he was strict and very, very proper, we all liked him and were fascinated by his British accent and the stories he told of his boyhood days in London. And every morning he would lead us in singing "God Save the King," followed by "O Canada."

Pinky took me to school every day. Mama didn't think I was old enough to walk the three miles across the prairie all by myself.

"When Joey starts school and there are two of you, then you won't need Pinky," she said.

In the meantime, Pinky and I usually went on horseback. I would ride behind him, holding my books and tin lunch pail. Sometimes, when Pinky had errands in town, we went in the wagon. And when it snowed, we always traveled by sleigh. That was fun, but I was still looking forward to bad weather and snowstorms and a vacation from school!

In preparation for the coming blizzards, Pinky

hauled in armloads of firewood, piling them up to the ceiling in the space behind the stove. And he laid a large piece of canvas over the stacks of wood outside the kitchen door to keep them dry.

Then he and Papa stretched a rope from the house to the barn.

"This way, even in the worst blizzard, we can follow the rope and not get lost when we go out to tend the animals," Pinky explained.

They moved the chicken coop into the barn, too, to the far end where the cows were. The heat from the cows' bodies and breath would keep the chickens warm.

And Pinky built a small pigsty beside the chicken coop. The pigs seemed content in their new indoor home, grunting happily and settling themselves in the fresh, clean straw.

Then Pinky rolled in barrels of barley mash. That's what the pigs liked to eat. They'd squeal and crowd around the trough every morning when Pinky ladled it out. We'd add table scraps to it, too, every day, for a treat.

It had been a good year for haying. Haystacks

dotted our pastures. Papa and Pinky forked large piles of hay into the corner of the barn by the horse stalls.

The cackles and moos, grunts and neighs, and the warmth of all the animals' bodies made the barn seem a very cheerful and cozy place.

When the work was finished, Papa rubbed his hands together in satisfaction. "Now we're ready for those blizzards you've been predicting, Pinky."

"No, not yet," said Mama. "First Pinky must move into the house."

Right away Pinky started to argue, saying he would be all right out in the bunkhouse, but Mama insisted. So he gathered up his few belongings and carried them into the storeroom that lay just beyond the kitchen.

The storeroom was small, but it was clean and warm. A metal cot stood along one wall, with a table holding a kerosene lamp at its head. In the middle of the room was a trapdoor leading to the root cellar, where we kept barrels of apples, turnips, and potatoes.

"When I lie on my cot, I can smell apples," Pinky

said, delighted, revealing the gold tooth he was so proud of in a grin that spread across his broad face. "It will be just like sleeping in an apple orchard in the summertime."

A few days later, the first blizzard struck. I remember it so clearly. It was on a Saturday, and Joey and I were helping Mama with the baking when it happened. One minute the sun was shining. The next, it was as dark as twilight outside.

Papa and Pinky rushed in from the barn.

"It's coming," said Papa. "Listen."

We all stood quietly in the kitchen and listened. Suddenly the snow began to pelt against the house with a fierce, lashing beat.

Mama quickly lit a kerosene lamp and placed it on the kitchen table. She seemed frightened. Her shadow, cast by the lamplight, loomed large on the wall. It wavered. She was trembling.

Joey went over to her and put his arms around her waist.

"Don't be afraid, Mama," he said, trying to sound just like Papa. "It will stop soon."

But it didn't.

For three long days, the wind howled and the

snow hammered at the walls of our house, blowing high snowdrifts into the yard and covering the outbuildings in a heavy, white blanket. The windowpanes were painted with thick frost. We had to thaw holes in it with our breath to look out.

Then, in the late afternoon of the third day, the wind uttered a final sob and died as suddenly as it had come. The snow stopped falling. A vast stillness settled over the prairie, and the sun emerged, shining dimly in the grey sky and casting a strange, brooding light over the land.

After supper, Papa went out to the barn to tend to the livestock.

"I don't know what's gotten into the animals," he told us when he returned. "They were fine during the blizzard, but now they're acting skittish. Perhaps all the quiet now that the winds have died down has affected them. The moon's come up, too—a bright, full moon. I almost didn't need my lantern to find my way back to the house."

Mama didn't answer. Her head was up, and she seemed to be listening to some distant sound.

And then we all heard it. From far across the prairie came the long, mournful howl of a wolf.

·The·Wolves·

The sound came again, rolling across the breathlessly silent prairie toward us—a long, drawn-out howl, low and mournful at first, then growing higher, shriller, and more desperate before it broke off abruptly into a series of frantic barks.

Mama was still standing by the stove, motionless, listening.

In the lamplight, Pinky's normally pale face had an almost greenish cast to it. *"Vohlk,"* he murmured in Russian. "A wolf," he said, shuddering. "And where there's one, there will be more."

He nervously fingered the silver pendant that hung from a thin chain around his neck. I knew what it was because he'd shown it to me many times. It was his Saint Mikhail medal, which pictured a man with wings holding a spear to the throat of a winged serpent.

"I pray to Saint Mikhail," Pinky always told me, "because it was he who cast the Dark One down from heaven and is fighting him still."

The wolf howled again. This time he was joined by a whole chorus of wailing. At the sound, I could feel the hairs on my arms begin to rise, and I remembered what Mrs. Kopek had said: that the wolves sounded like lost souls, crying to God. I looked over at Mama. She was trembling.

"There must be at least a dozen of them out there," Pinky said.

"Oh, come now," Papa said briskly, with an anxious glance at Mama, who flinched and quivered at each new burst of howling. "There's nothing to worry about. Those wolves are miles away. Now that the storm has ended, they will go back

where they came from. Wolves don't stay in settled areas. They are just as afraid of us as we are
of them."

"That is not so," Pinky replied, shaking his head.
"In Russia—"

"I don't want to hear any of your Russian folktales about wolves chasing people over the snow,"
Papa said firmly. "This isn't Russia. It's Canada,
where no wolves have ever harmed anyone."

"But—" protested Pinky.

"Please, Pinky," Papa said. "You'll frighten the
children."

Mama looked around the kitchen and gave herself a brisk little shake. "And I am being the big-
gest child of all, aren't I? Anthony is right, Pinky.
The wolves mean us no harm. They will leave
soon, I'm sure."

But the wolves were still howling when I went up
the steep, enclosed staircase to bed that night.

Our home was large for a wooden house on
a treeless prairie, where lumber had to be spe-
cial-ordered and brought in either by train or

oxcart. The house had been small at first, but
Papa had added on to it after he and Mama
were married and his first harvest had come in.

Not only did we have three upstairs bedrooms,
but we also had a small sewing room for Mama.
It had originally been used as a nursery, first for
me and then for Joey. Mama and Papa's bedroom
was at one end of the house. Next to it was the
sewing room, then Joey's room. Mine was last, a
corner room, on the opposite end of the house
from Mama and Papa's.

All the bedrooms opened out onto a long hall
that ran the front width of the house. Its three
windows let in the sunshine by day and the moonlight by night.

The hall was usually a cheerful place with its
views of sunrises and sunsets and green fields. But
tonight, as I walked its moonlit length to my room,
it seemed . . . different. Shadowy. Threatening. I
began to tiptoe, as if afraid someone or something
terrible was listening for me, waiting for me in the
dark.

Then, silently scolding myself for acting like a

baby, I deliberately made myself stop before one of the windows, pull back the curtain to banish the shadows, and look out.

There was a full moon that night. I stared up at it, almost expecting to see the dark profile of a howling wolf against its silvery roundness, the way wolves are always pictured in storybooks. But there was only the cold moon shining down on the prairie.

And the howling of unseen creatures.

The sound seemed to come in waves, with all the wolves joining in, sending their cries higher and higher—wilder, more eerie—before their howls peaked and crested and broke into that awful, shrill barking and yipping.

Then a few seconds of silence and it would start all over again.

I tried not to listen to the wolves as I crawled between the icy sheets of my bed, but the still night air carried the sound, making them seem close, so close.

I huddled beneath the covers, drawing my knees up and wrapping my arms around me. I was just beginning to create a warm spot for myself in the center of the bed when a small figure appeared in the doorway that connected Joey's room with mine.

"I thought you might want me to sleep with you tonight, Therese," Joey said in a quavering voice. "You must be very frightened."

I smiled in the darkness as Joey crawled in beside me. The folds of his long flannel nightgown felt cold, and his plump little body was trembling.

"Thank you, Joey. I'll sleep better, now that you're here to protect me."

When Joey's even breathing told me he had fallen asleep, I closed my eyes and drifted off, too.

Later—it must have been after midnight—I awoke. Someone was pacing up and down the hall. I crept softly to the door and looked out. It was Mama, in her long, white flannel nightgown. Her pale hair streamed down her back. In the moonlight, she looked like a lost angel.

"Mama?" I whispered, so as not to wake Joey. "What is it, Mama?"

She paused briefly, then resumed her pacing— up and down, up and down the hall.

"Mama?" I repeated. "Is something wrong?"

Her eyes were open, but she didn't seem to see me. Mrs. Kopek had told me stories about sleep-walkers, and how you must never awaken them, so I stood quietly and watched.

Mama stopped pacing and drifted over to the window. Although she appeared to be looking out, her eyes were blank and silvery.

A little shudder ran over her body at each new chorus of howls from the distant wolf pack. Once I saw her fumble at the window, as if she intended to throw it open, but then her hand fell back, lifeless, to her side.

I don't know how long I stood there, my bare feet numb with cold, watching her.

At last the howling stopped. Mama remained at the window for a few more moments, then turned and went back to her room.

The next morning, with the sun shining on the bright, glistening snow, what I'd seen in the night seemed like a dream.

I dressed quickly and hurried down to the kitchen.

Joey was already at the table, happily eating flapjacks. A sticky little trail of maple syrup ran from the corner of his mouth down to his chin.

Mama was at the stove, flipping another batch. She was wearing a clean, starched apron, and her hair was up in a bun. She looked very sensible and motherly. Nothing at all like the pale, haunted sleepwalker of the previous night.

"I'm sorry I'm late for breakfast, Mama. I must have overslept."

My mother looked over at me and smiled. "I'm glad you slept so soundly, Therese. I didn't. I had such strange nightmares. Something about the wolves. I think I dreamed they were calling to me."

She placed a steaming pile of flapjacks on a plate and handed it to me.

"I must have gone to sleep remembering those terrible wolf stories Pinky likes to tell," she continued. "I guess the howling frightened me. This is the first time wolves have come this far south. I've never heard such sounds before."

I wanted to ask her if she knew she'd been

sleepwalking last night. And why she didn't remember that the wolves had come down from the north thirteen years ago, the winter she'd appeared at Mrs. Kopek's door.

But something held me back. Maybe I was remembering how Mrs. Kopek had said that it might upset Mama to ask her about that part of her past. She never spoke of it, so maybe it was something she didn't like to think about.

Besides, I knew Mama was worried about those wolves. If I told her I'd seen her pacing the hall last night in her sleep, it would worry her even more. It would be just one more thing she couldn't remember. So I didn't say anything and hoped it wouldn't happen again.

Mama took a pan of hot water and a cloth and thawed the frost from the kitchen windows to let in the sun. From my seat at the table, I could look out and watch Papa and Pinky watering the cows.

"It must be terribly cold out there," I commented. "Papa and Pinky keep swinging their arms to keep warm. And their faces are red!"

Pinky was wearing the smoked glasses a doctor

in Regina had made up for him. The sun hurt Pinky's pale eyes, especially in the winter when it glittered on the snow.

I saw him break the ice on the watering trough and lead the cows to it. The cows walked like old women, humped over and shivering in the cold. They drank in dainty sips, holding their mouths as though the cold water hurt their teeth.

"Oh look, Mama," I cried. "Who's that coming across the pasture? Is it Mrs. Kopek?"

Mama went to the window and looked out. Then she began to laugh. "Yes, and she's wearing her visiting clothes. But look at her feet, Therese!"

"Let me see! I want to see, too," Joey cried, pushing his chair back. The two of us joined Mama at the window.

Mrs. Kopek was a comical sight. She had on her black seal-fur coat and matching hat, and she carried her muff. But she was wearing a pair of heavy boots, strapped into her husband's old snowshoes. She made rapid progress as she crossed the field toward our house.

"She looks excited," I said, "as though she has something she's bursting to tell us."

FOUR

▪ Mr. ▪ Hoffmeister's ▪ Ride ▪

God bless this house and all who ˙dwell within," Mrs. Kopek declared in ringing tones as she entered the kitchen. She never came into a house without saying that.

Then she carefully removed her fur coat and draped it over a chair, blowing on the collar a little to raise the hairs. She took off her hat, as though she were lifting a crown from her head, and sat it on the windowsill. It lay there like a black cat crouching and warming itself in the sun.

When Mama pulled out a kitchen chair, Mrs. Kopek seated herself in it, her back straight, head erect, and hands folded in her lap. She looked quite regal, like the pictures of King Edward's mother, Queen Victoria, sitting on her throne. Mrs. Kopek was prettier, though, even in her stocking feet. She'd taken off her boots and snowshoes outside the door.

Mama got out her best teapot and threw in a generous pinch of tea leaves. Mrs. Kopek liked her tea strong. Then Mama put the kettle on to boil and joined Mrs. Kopek at the table.

"What a story I have to tell, my dears," Mrs. Kopek said importantly. "But first, my tea. The trip across the field has given me a cough."

I waited impatiently as the kettle water came to a boil. Then Mama steeped the tea leaves in the pot and poured the tea. Mrs. Kopek held a lump of sugar in her front teeth, Russian style, and sucked the tea through it. Joey stared at her in fascination.

"Bad for the teeth," she told him, "but sweet in the throat."

"What has happened, Mrs. Kopek?" Mama asked. "Have you received a letter from one of your sons? Is something wrong?"

Mrs. Kopek waved her hand and chuckled. "My sons are as strong as plow horses. Nothing is ever wrong with them. But old Mr. Hoffmeister and his wife—ah, now, that is something else." She stopped and drank deeply from her teacup.

"Oh dear, the Hoffmeisters," Mama said worriedly. "I've been thinking about them. I hope they were able to do their chores in this blizzard. They're really too old for farming."

"No, my dear, they had no problems getting their chores done." Mrs. Kopek smiled playfully, prolonging the suspense. "Oh, no. It was much more serious than that."

Mama sighed. She knew Mrs. Kopek as well as I did.

"Is Mr. Hoffmeister sick?" she prompted. "Or is Mrs. Hoffmeister having trouble with her back again?"

Mrs. Kopek set her cup down and leaned forward over the table, locking eyes with Mama.

"Mr. Hoffmeister," she said, speaking slowly and enunciating every word, "nearly died in the blizzard. And it was only by the grace of God that poor Mrs. Hoffmeister escaped a heart attack!"

Mama gasped and pressed her hands to her mouth.

Seeing her stricken look, Mrs. Kopek leaned back in her chair, satisfied that she'd successfully launched her tale.

"Mr. Hoffmeister," she continued, "had gone into town the day of the blizzard. The weather was cold but sunny when he set off, with little snow on the ground, so he took his wagon. He told his wife he would be home long before dark.

"But late in the afternoon, when the winds rose and the snows blasted across the prairie, he still hadn't returned. Mrs. Hoffmeister was beside herself with worry. She realized her husband must have been halfway home when the blizzard struck. Would he try to get back to town? No, she decided. He'd probably push on for home.

"So she placed a lamp in the window, as a bea-

con, turning the wick up as high as it would go,"
Mrs. Kopek said. "She hoped he might be able to
see the light through the storm and that it would
guide him home. The snow was almost blinding
at this point, but it was all she could think of
to do.

"Then she paced the floor, back and forth, back
and forth.

"Suddenly her dog, who'd been dozing by the
stove, jumped up and began to bark. Mrs. Hoffmeister rushed to the window and looked out. She
heard the faint rumble of the wagon as it went
past the door, headed for the barn. And through
the blowing snow she could just barely make out
a faint light swinging to and fro. It was Mr. Hoffmeister's wagon lantern. The wagon seemed to be
moving at a rapid clip."

She paused to explain. "Those Hoffmeister
horses are steady, sensible animals. How they ever
made it home from town in that blizzard, I'll never
know. And now they were in a hurry to reach the
barn."

"And to think," Mama said with a shiver, "that

we were all safe and warm here in our kitchen when poor Mr. Hoffmeister was out in the blizzard!"

Mrs. Kopek took another sip of her tea and continued.

"Mrs. Hoffmeister threw a heavy shawl over her head and struggled out through the wind and snow to the barn. She had to make her way slowly, close to the house, for fear of getting lost. Then she followed the bushes that lined the pathway to the barn."

"Pinky put up a rope so *we* couldn't get lost in a storm," Joey said. "The Hoffmeisters should have done it, too."

"Don't interrupt, Joey," Mama said gently.

Mrs. Kopek quelled Joey with a frown.

"Children should be seen but not heard," she said sternly. "Now, let me see. Where was I? Ah, yes. Well, when she reached the barn, Mrs. Hoffmeister found her husband sitting upright in the wagon. His eyebrows and beard were covered with ice, and his clothes were thick with snow. At first she thought he was a corpse—a frozen corpse. She said that's when she nearly had a heart attack, poor woman."

"But Mr. Hoffmeister wasn't dead, was he?" Mama put in anxiously.

"No, no. Mrs. Hoffmeister shouted at him, calling his name, then climbed up on the seat beside him and shook him.

"He finally roused himself and, with his wife's help, climbed down from the wagon. After Mrs. Hoffmeister unhitched the horses—who were in a terrible state, stamping and trembling—and had thrown blankets over them, she helped her husband start back toward the house.

"They sank and floundered many times in the snow, but finally, thanks to the lamp in the window, they made it to the door. Mrs. Hoffmeister thrust Mr. Hoffmeister into a kitchen chair and forced brandy down his throat. Little by little, he thawed out."

"Thank heaven!" Mama exclaimed.

"And when he was himself once again," Mrs. Kopek said, "he told the most fearful story."

"I can well imagine," Mama said. "It must have

been a terrible trip home through the blizzard."

"Oh no, my dear," said Mrs. Kopek. "It was more than that. Mr. Hoffmeister said he was trailed by a pack of wolves."

"Wolves?" Mama and I said the word almost at the same time. *"Wolves?"*

Joey jumped down from his chair and ran over to Mama. I don't know if he did it because he was frightened or because he thought he had to comfort her. Probably a little of both. He put his arms around her waist. "Wolves?" he echoed.

"Didn't you hear them last night, howling like demons?" Mrs. Kopek asked.

"Yes," Mama said, almost in a whisper. Her lips were grey, and her eyes wide. "But Anthony said . . . we thought they were miles away."

"Perhaps they were, later," said Mrs. Kopek. "But first they followed poor Mr. Hoffmeister nearly to his door."

"But wolves won't come near people," I said, parroting Papa. "They're just as afraid of us as we are of them."

"Oh, is that so, Miss Know-it-all?" Mrs. Kopek

asked, looking haughtily down her nose at me. "Then tell that to the Hoffmeisters' hired man, who'd been in his bunkhouse, snug as a turtle, during the blizzard. He didn't find out what had happened until later that evening, when he managed to make it to the house. He came by my place this morning and told me the whole story. And he swore to me that everything he said was true. Mr. Hoffmeister had indeed been chased by wolves!"

I'd heard the expression "my blood ran cold." Now I knew what it meant. Actually, I felt like someone had just poured ice water into my veins. I could feel it start somewhere around my heart and go downhill, through the rest of my body.

Mrs. Kopek resumed her tale.

"Mr. Hoffmeister was a short distance from home when the blizzard struck. He figured he'd be all right, since the horses knew the way, so he slackened the reins and let them guide the wagon as best they could.

"Suddenly the horses pulled up short and began to whinny and dance sideways. 'Steady now,' he called out to them, but they only reared and plunged."

Mrs. Kopek narrowed her eyes, and her voice became lower, huskier. I leaned forward so I wouldn't miss a word.

"Suddenly Mr. Hoffmeister became aware of dark shapes moving in the snow beside the wagon. He leaned over and looked, and what he saw turned him rigid with fright."

"The wolves," I gasped.

"Nearly a dozen of them," said Mrs. Kopek, "ringed around the wagon. Silent. Walking low to the ground, like shadows."

Mama shuddered. Joey crawled up in her lap. He hadn't done that in a long time.

"Mr. Hoffmeister took a tight grip on the reins and forced the horses to continue at a slow walk. He was afraid that if he gave them their heads, they would begin to run and the wolves would give chase and attack them.

"It was a slow trip home. The wolves never left the wagon's side. Several times the horses floundered and led the wagon into a ditch. Mr. Hoffmeister had to climb down and then lead them back up to the road. And all the while he had to hold on to the reins for dear life, because those horses wanted so badly to run away."

"Wasn't he scared?" I asked. Just thinking about being that close to a pack of wolves made my hands shake.

"Yes, but there was nothing else he could do. He knew he couldn't make it home without the horses; he'd freeze to death in the blizzard before he'd gone a couple of miles. And besides, he couldn't just go off and leave them in a ditch to die or be eaten by the wolves."

"But the wolves didn't attack the horses," Mama said faintly.

"No. Maybe they won't attack animals when there's a human around. Who knows? Anyway, those wolves just stood there, waiting for him. Each time he got down from the wagon, he was afraid they might change their minds and go for his throat.

"Finally, when he reached the farmyard and was close enough to the house to see the dim light of the lamp Mrs. Hoffmeister had placed in the window, the wolves left him. He said they simply faded away into the blizzard.

"Once he was sure the wolves were gone, Mr. Hoffmeister slapped the reins on the horses' backs, and they ran lickety-split for the barn. And that's where Mrs. Hoffmeister found him, speechless and half-dead with fright and cold. She said he was trembling so violently that she had to half-drag, half-carry him down from the wagon seat, and her such a skinny little thing, too."

Mrs. Kopek surveyed our pale, frightened faces with satisfaction. She picked an imaginary thread off the bosom of her black dress and pretended to examine her fingernails.

Her eyes glowed. This had been one of her best, her finest, moments as a storyteller.

"Yes," she said, "a pack of wolves followed poor Mr. Hoffmeister home through a blizzard, and he lived to tell the tale. And now, my dear, may I please have another cup of tea?"

FIVE

·The·Sleepwalker·

The next morning, Papa hitched the horses to the sleigh and went into town.

"Please, Papa, take me with you," Joey had begged.

"No, Joey. The weather might change. You stay here and take care of Mama and Therese."

When he returned, Papa told us that everyone was talking about Mr. Hoffmeister and the wolves.

"Not only did those wolves follow Mr. Hoffmeister," he said, "but apparently they made several raids on livestock in the area. They broke into the Farnams' barn and killed a young heifer, and the Magnusens' barn, which was bolted securely, had claw marks on the door. Those wolves are hungry, no doubt about it. With such good pickings in this area, it looks as if they intend to stick around for a while."

"Isn't there anything we can do?" Mama asked.

"Some of the men were talking about arming themselves and going out to hunt them," Papa told her. "I said I'd join them. We'll go tomorrow if the weather holds. In the meantime, though, we must keep the barn door barred at all times and do all the outdoor chores before nightfall."

But the next morning another blizzard struck, so the men couldn't go out on their hunt. And just when it had blown itself out, another came sweeping down on us from the north. And then another.

For over a week the wind shrieked and shrieked, and the snow lashed angrily at the house, rattling the dishes on the shelves. It was hard to remember when the prairie had been silent, with only the honking of the wild geese and the song of the meadowlark to break its stillness.

I worried about Papa and Pinky every time they

staggered out through the driving snow to tend the animals. What if a pack of wolves suddenly appeared and surrounded them, the way they had Mr. Hoffmeister?

I worried about the brooding presence of the wolves. Their howling could not be heard over the wail of the wind, but I knew they were still out there. I don't know how I knew that, but I did. It was that same prickly feeling you get when someone behind you is staring at the back of your neck. That's how I felt about the wolves, although I tried to tell myself I was just imagining things.

Mostly, though, I worried about Mama.

I'd gotten in the habit of secretly watching her as we moved through the house each day, dusting and straightening. She'd grown pale and jittery, and she jumped at every sudden noise. She didn't talk much now, either, and always seemed to be listening for something. Her head would go up, and a faraway look would come into her eyes. Then she'd stop whatever she was doing and listen . . . just listen.

What does she hear? I wondered. The wind? Is she listening to the wind?

I tried to talk to Papa about it. I didn't know what else to do. I knew I couldn't ask Mama what was wrong. She'd never been one to talk about what was going on in her mind, and now she was even more reserved.

Talking to Papa didn't get me anywhere. Maybe I explained it badly, I don't know. Papa only ruffled my hair and said, "Cabin fever, Therese. Your Mama is a very delicate and sensitive woman. Many women of her temperament get that way when they've been penned up for days, as Mama has."

I should have guessed that Papa wouldn't think Mama's "cabin fever" was anything to get upset about. He was a practical, no-nonsense sort of person. For him, life was quite simple. As he always said, "I do what I can, and I don't worry about the things I can't change. That's why I sleep like a log at night. Nothing rouses me, and I dream no dreams."

And so, when Mama began sleepwalking again,

he never heard her. I did, though. Night after night I heard her pacing up and down the hall. I would lie there in the dark, listening.

Once she even made her way down to the kitchen. When I heard her begin to go down the stairs, I slipped out of bed and followed her, worried that she might fall and hurt herself.

I stayed a little behind her, not wanting to wake her, and remained on the stairs as she entered the kitchen. I didn't know what else to do.

I heard the thud of a chair as she bumped into it, then a rattling as she unbolted the back door. I was about to fly down the stairs and stop her from walking out into the blizzard when Pinky's door creaked open.

"Madam," I heard him say in that polite, respectful voice he always used with Mama. "Where are you going?"

There was a brief silence. Then Mama's puzzled voice floated up to me.

"I . . . I . . . don't know, Pinky. I was having this strange dream, you see. It was all so real. The wolves were calling to me."

Another silence. Then Pinky said, and he sounded frightened, "Yes, of course. We all sleep uneasily these nights, but you must return to bed. All will be well in the morning."

I padded down the stairs, stepped silently into the kitchen, and stood watching.

The kitchen was in darkness, except for flickering patches of light when the wind blew swirling rags of snow across the pathway of the moon.

Mama was a white blur in the darkness as she stood hesitantly before the door. The shadowy bulk that was Pinky moved to the window, and I saw him pluck nervously at his Saint Mikhail medal, gleaming silver in the moonlight. He always touched it, rotating it with his fingers, when he was nervous.

Mama shoved the bolt on the back door, locking it again, then turned and said, "Thank you, Pinky." She was speaking in normal tones now. "I can't imagine what I thought I was doing."

"It was just the wind," Pinky assured her, although there was still that odd note of fear in his voice. "It does strange things to the nerves."

"Yes, that's what it must have been—the wind," Mama said. Then, "You won't say anything about this to Anthony, will you? It will only worry him."

"No, if you'd rather I didn't," Pinky replied hesitantly. "But—"

"Please . . . please don't."

"Whatever you say, Madam."

"Thank you, Pinky. I appreciate that."

Then Mama left the kitchen and slowly mounted the stairs.

I was standing in the corner by the stove. I guess she couldn't see me in the shadows, and I didn't know whether to let her know I was there. But I decided that if she didn't want Papa to know about her sleepwalking, she probably didn't want me to know about it, either.

Pinky was still standing in front of the window, clutching his Saint Mikhail medal. I was going to say something to him, ask him about Mama's sleepwalking, when I saw him drop down on one knee, make the sign of the cross on his breast, and begin to pray.

He prayed aloud, but in a soft, whispery voice,

and I could only recognize one word, repeated at intervals, in the Russian phrases.

I realized, with a guilty start, that I shouldn't be standing there watching him, listening to him. I was eavesdropping, and on his prayers, too, which made it even worse. I turned and went quickly up the stairs, my bare feet making no sound.

As I climbed into bed, I wondered what Pinky was praying for. He'd seemed very earnest.

And why had he kept saying the word for *wolf* over and over again in his prayers?

▪The▪White▪Wolf▪

The blizzard ended before daybreak, and the sun rose, hanging flat and silvery behind the grey clouds.

Papa prepared to go into town again. This time he took his rifle down from the rack beside the kitchen door and filled his pockets with cartridges.

"The hunting party will be gathering soon at Povich's general store," he stold Mama, "and they'll need every man they can get. I'm hoping we can muster up a good-sized group, especially if those wolves have broken into any more barns."

He buttoned his fleece-lined jacket slowly, a frown puckering his brows.

"I just wish they hadn't let Povich take charge of the wolf hunt. I've never liked that man. He has a mean streak in him."

I knew what Papa meant. I didn't like Mr. Povich either. There *was* a mean streak in him. You could see it in the way he held his thin, lipless little mouth pinched tight, and the rough, rude way he talked to his wife and his timid little daughters. One was my age, and she was scared of her own shadow. No wonder!

But Mr. Povich was an important man in our community, and a powerful one. He owned the only general store for miles around, so all the local families either had to buy from him or do without.

He could be spiteful, too. Once he got mad at one of our neighbors and pretended to be out of stock when the man tried to buy a harness. Our neighbor had to travel miles to find another like the one Mr. Povich had hidden on his back shelf. Mr. Povich laughed and bragged about it later, as though proud of what he had done.

And hadn't Mrs. Kopek told me that Mr. Povich had never forgiven Mrs. Povich for her failure to give him a son? He acted like it was all her fault, something she was doing just to torment him.

"Who let Mr. Povich take charge of the hunt?" Mama asked.

"No one, really. He just always sets himself up as the leader, and who's going to tell him otherwise? We all need him and his store more than he needs us."

He slung his rifle over his shoulder and bent down to kiss Mama.

"But Anthony," she said, "shouldn't Pinky go with you?"

"No," Papa replied. "I want him to stay here, with you. And tell him not to forget to take one of the rifles with him whenever he goes out to the barn. Who knows where those wolves are going to turn up next?"

Then he patted my cheek with a gloved hand and was gone.

The afternoon dragged by. Mama helped me with my lessons, since there would be no school until the weather improved. I tried to tell her it was a holiday and I shouldn't have to do homework, but she was dead set on my not wasting time.

She helped me try to memorize a poem about the wreck of a famous ship, but my mind wasn't on it. I'd never seen a ship. I'd never seen an ocean. It was hard to imagine what one was really like, although I'd seen pictures in books. I was used to the prairie. That was my ocean—miles and miles of flat land, with the edge of the horizon way off in the distance.

Together, the two of us tried to teach Joey the alphabet, but he was as bad as I was. Joey wasn't thinking about learning to read. He was off in his imagination with Papa, hunting wolves.

Although Pinky came in and out of the kitchen, neither he nor Mama said a word about what had happened the night before. They seemed to be avoiding each other's gaze. I wondered about this, but I didn't say anything, and I pretended not to notice the strangeness between them. I was still young enough to think that adults always knew what was best.

Finally, just before twilight, Papa came home.

"They're gone," he said, sitting down before the stove and pulling off his boots. He stretched his feet out toward the warmth of the fire and leaned back in his chair with a deep sigh.

"There were fifteen of us. We divided up into search parties and rode out in all directions, sweeping the countryside. No one could find a trace of them. It was like looking for ghosts."

Pinky muttered something in Russian.

"What's that? Speak English, Pinky," Papa said sharply. He was irritable from fatigue.

"I said, you won't find them because they don't want you to."

Papa snorted. "Nonsense. Now that the weather has cleared, they've probably headed back up north, and good riddance."

But later that night, when we were all in bed, the howling began again.

I pulled my pillow over my ears to shut out the sound.

If Mama paced the hall, I didn't want to hear it. All this was beyond me. I no longer wanted any part of it. If I ignored the unpleasant things that were happening, perhaps they would go away and life would be happy and cozy again, just as it was before the wolves came.

Papa, Mama, and Pinky were already at breakfast when I came down the next morning.

"For the last time, Pinky," Papa was saying, "let's get this straight. This is real life, not some crazy Russian folktale. Yes, I know, those wolves are still hanging around, but it won't be for long. They'll soon find out we're not going to let them have our livestock. When they've been shot at a couple of times, they'll clear out, believe me. So in the meantime, we go about our business as usual."

In the days that followed, I almost forgot about the wolves. The weather cleared and the sun shone, although the snow still lay, bright and glittering, on the ground.

There's a passage in the Bible about shadows fleeing away when the day breaks. That's how I felt, now that the blizzards had ended and we were having sunny days.

If the wolves were still out there on some distant, icy knoll, who cared? They weren't letting anybody know it. They'd stopped howling at night, and none of our neighbors had reported any attempted raids on their livestock.

School reopened. Pinky drove me back and forth to the little one-room schoolhouse every day in the sleigh, his rifle propped beside him on the seat.

My friends all talked about the blizzards, of course, and the wolves. Most of the bigger boys thought the howling was exciting. They liked it and wished it would start up again so that there would be another wolf hunt. They said they were going to ask their fathers if they could go on the next one, and acted like they'd be allowed to, but I knew it was just talk.

All the children talked a lot about those wolves. You'd think nothing interesting had ever happened to them before. Well, come to think of it, maybe nothing ever had.

My good friend Alice told me in a whisper that her mother was really afraid of the wolves and that the howling had nearly driven her crazy.

That made me feel better about Mama. Maybe she wasn't any different from a lot of other
homesteaders' wives. Maybe Papa was right.
Maybe Mama just had a bad case of "cabin
fever." She still looked pale and anxious, but I
was sure that would go away once the wolves
moved off for good.

Several weeks passed. Although we had no more
snowstorms, the temperature was below freezing,
and the snowdrifts hardened where they lay.

Our neighbors had all begun to relax about the
wolves. Although they still walked around carrying rifles, they said they probably wouldn't have
to use them after all.

And then a full moon rose, and it all began
again: first, the howling, then the wolf hunts—
the wolves eluding the hunters—and Mama's
nightly pacing in the hall.

That was when the white wolf first appeared.

Mrs. Kopek brought us the news.

I arrived home from school one day and found
her in the kitchen, talking to Mama. Joey wasn't

there. He must have been up in his room, taking a nap.

"A white wolf!" Mrs. Kopek was exclaiming, her teacup rattling in her hand. "Mr. Povich saw it last night, scratching at his barn door. He shot at it but missed, the silly fool, and it got away."

Mama froze in the act of putting the teakettle on the stove.

"Was the white wolf alone?"

"No. Mr. Povich says there were others, lurking in the shadows. But he thinks the white one is their leader."

"Why does he think that?" Mama asked in a faint voice.

"Because it seemed to give the others a kind of signal, which they obeyed," replied Mrs. Kopek. "Wolves always have a leader."

Pinky had come into the kitchen and was listening, standing quietly by the stove.

"So the white one has finally joined them," he said.

"What do you mean, *finally*?" I demanded. I

could see they were upsetting Mama again, and it made me angry.

Pinky ignored me and turned to Mrs. Kopek. "You are a Russian, Mrs. Kopek. You know the legends."

Mrs. Kopek shifted uneasily in her chair. "Yes, I'm a Russian, but I left all that foolishness behind me in the old country. And you should have too, Pinky. This is a new land. People here are practical and sensible. They don't believe in silly superstitions, thank God."

"What kind of superstitions?" I asked. "What are you talking about, Pinky?"

"I'm talking about the white wolf and what it means when one appears," Pinky said.

Mama sat down at the table and looked at me uncertainly. "Therese, dear, perhaps you ought to go upstairs and do your homework."

I stood my ground. "No, Mama, I'm old enough now to know what's happening." I sounded just like Papa when I said that.

Mrs. Kopek nodded her approval. Hadn't she always treated me like a grown-up?

"Let her stay, my dear," she said, reaching across the table and patting Mama's hand. "Children should be a part of things. They only listen in corners otherwise."

She turned to Pinky. "And now, what is all this nonsense you're spouting?"

"You know what it means when the white wolf comes," Pinky repeated stubbornly.

Mrs. Kopek shuffled her feet impatiently beneath the table. "Wolves come in different colors, Pinky. If the leader of the pack is white, so what? It signifies nothing."

"No. This is the thirteenth year, isn't it? And every thirteenth year—"

"I don't know what all this is about," Mama said. Her voice was a little unsteady. "Thirteenth year? Is this some kind of riddle, Pinky?"

"I wish it were," Pinky replied. "But Mrs. Kopek, who comes from my country, knows what it means when a white wolf appears once every thirteenth year."

"Yes, yes, I know the old legend. And that's all it is—a legend." Mrs. Kopek rolled her eyes eloquently. "It's supposed to mean that the white wolf is . . . Oh, this is ridiculous, Pinky."

"Say it," commanded Pinky. "When a white wolf appears in the thirteenth year, it is—"

"It is a half human. A werewolf." Mrs. Kopek finished the sentence and sighed. "And it's been thirteen years since the wolves last came. But, Pinky, there *was* no white wolf the other time."

"Oh no? People say there was. Ask Mr. Lindstrom. He says he saw it with his own eyes."

"Mr. Lindstrom is a fool," Mrs. Kopek retorted. "Any white wolf he saw came from the bottle we all know he drinks from."

"There was a white wolf then," Pinky insisted. "And there is a white wolf now. A half human. Someone able to assume the shape and animal nature of a wolf."

"Pinky, no! This can't be possible—can it?" Mama cried.

I waited for Pinky to answer Mama, to tell her that maybe he was wrong, after all. That Mrs.

Kopek was probably right. That it *was* all just a lot of silly superstition. Or that he was only joking. Anything to erase what he had said.

But Pinky didn't reply. He turned on his heel and left the kitchen.

SEVEN

▪The▪Night▪
of▪the▪Hunters▪

Mama drifted about the house after Mrs. Kopek
left, picking things up, staring at them, and then
putting them down again.

When Joey or I spoke to her, she seemed to
pull herself back from some faraway place in her
mind in order to answer us.

When Papa got home, I saw him eyeing her
anxiously. I knew he was thinking that Mama's
cabin fever was growing worse.

Mrs. Kopek had explained "cabin fever" to me
once. She said it was a terrible, black depression,

and that a lot of the settlers' wives got it, back when nobody had any close neighbors. It was caused by loneliness, and the dismal, howling sound the wind made as it came sweeping across the prairie, she said.

I guess Papa finally had started worrying about Mama because he now told her, "Let's hitch up the sleigh and drive into town tomorrow. We'll take the children. Maybe there's something you want to buy for yourself at the general store. A new shawl, or a length of dress fabric, maybe. Would you like that?"

"What?" Mama replied absently. "Oh . . . yes, Anthony. Thank you. That would be very nice."

"I'd like a bag of rock candy and a slingshot," Joey piped up. "I can drive the wolves off with a slingshot, can't I, Papa?"

Papa laughed and ruffled Joey's soft, fine hair, although his eyes followed Mama as she went to the window and stared out over the prairie.

"What will you put in your slingshot, Joey?" he asked. "Candy? The pebbles are all buried under the snow, you know."

Joey thought for a moment. "No, I'll eat the candy and just pretend to shoot at the wolves."

Mama was wearing thick woolen stockings that day, stuffed into an old pair of Papa's slippers. It seemed strange to me, because she was always careful about her appearance and wore shoes about the house, not slippers.

I asked her about it as she stood at the window.

Without turning, she said, "Chilblains. I guess I must have had my feet too close to the fire."

I nodded sympathetically, knowing what chilblains were and how painful they could be. I'd had them last winter, when I played in the snow too long and nearly froze my feet. When I warmed up at the fire, my toes swelled and turned purple. Then they hurt and itched.

I heard a sound from the doorway. Pinky was standing there, holding a harness, the one he said needed to be oiled. He was staring at Mama's feet.

I saw his hand creep furtively to his neck and finger his silver medal.

What's wrong with him? I wondered. Why is he looking at Mama like that?

Ever since Mrs. Kopek had come over with her story of the white wolf, Pinky had been walking around with a long face, looking mysterious and clutching his medal of Saint Mikhail with a lance at the throat of the Dark One.

Dark One, indeed, I thought spitefully. It's Pinky, with his pale eyes and white hair, who'd been carrying on like the Dark One in *this* house!

I found it hard to get to sleep that night. When Mama began her usual pacing, I resolutely stuck my fingers in my ears and started reciting my multiplication tables. By the time I reached the eights, I'd fallen asleep.

Or at least I *think* I was asleep.

I dreamed—was it a dream? It seemed so real —that Mama slipped down the stairs and went out into the night. The cold, cold night.

I awoke to a thumping and banging. It seemed to go on forever. I finally realized that someone was pounding on the kitchen door.

Fully awake now, I grabbed my bathrobe and ran out into the hall.

The bright moonlight slanted in through the window, and I saw Papa come out of his room, stagger slightly, and hit his shoulder on the doorjamb. He was still half asleep.

"Go back to bed, Therese," he mumbled.

"Please, Papa," I said, "I want to see who it is!"

He didn't answer, so I figured that meant I could stay up.

Papa made his way down the stairs, and I followed closely, slipping into my robe as I went. Neither Mama nor Joey seemed to have awakened, since they didn't appear behind me. They must be sleeping soundly, I thought.

The knocking on the door continued. The person knocking seemed to be using both fists now and kicking at the door as well.

"Just a minute! Just a minute!" Papa called out.

I huddled close to the stove, shivering. We banked the fire every night, but the ashes still gave off a little heat.

Papa took the kerosene lamp from the table and, after several tries, managed to light it. Holding it high, he crossed the floor. A cold draft blew into the kitchen when he flung the back door open wide.

The clock on the wall told me it was two o'clock. It's strange, isn't it, how you notice unimportant things when something frightening is happening?

Mr. Povich and a group of men—neighbors and men from town—were gathered in the dooryard. They were carrying guns and torches. I could see the uneven flickering and flaming through the window.

Mr. Povich stuck his torch in a snowbank and shouldered his way into the kitchen, followed by several of the men closest to him.

"It's the white wolf," Mr. Povich said abruptly in his rasping, unpleasant voice. "It was headed this way, as far as we could tell."

Papa blinked and rubbed the back of his hand across his eyes. "What are you saying, Mr. Povich?" he asked. "You've just gotten me out of a dead sleep. What's going on here?"

"The white wolf and his filthy band broke into Findley's barn," Mr. Povich said. He gestured to the man behind him.

I knew Mr. Findley. He was nice. I went to school with his sons.

"They were attacking my horses," Mr. Findley put in. His voice quavered and he swallowed hard. "I heard the commotion, grabbed my rifle, and ran out. But they got poor old Blackie. He was down on his knees, screaming. I hope I never hear a sound like that again. The white wolf and two others were hanging from his neck by their jaws. It was a god-awful sight—blood everywhere! And that horse was my boys' pet, too. They all learned to ride on him." Mr. Findley was unable to continue.

"So Findley, here, started shooting," said Mr. Povich, taking up the tale. "He says he hit the white wolf in the front leg. He couldn't finish him off, though, because the other wolves closed ranks around their leader, just like trained soldiers. They all ran away, circling and protecting the white wolf, who was limping, with Mr. Findley firing after them."

Papa had been pulling on the pair of woolen trousers he kept on a hook by the door, yanking them on over his nightshirt and pulling up the suspenders. Now he grabbed his boots, which were drying before the stove, and stuffed his feet into them, tying the laces with trembling fingers.

"So, Mr. Findley took one of the other horses and rode to the Lindstrom farm," Mr. Povich continued. "We roused the Lindstrom boys, and they rode to the neighboring farms, rounding up a posse. We figured you'd want to join us."

Papa put on his fleece-lined jacket and picked up his rifle.

"You bet I do," he said. "But where do we start looking?"

"That's the bad part, I'm afraid." Mr. Povich looked down at his feet.

"We all know how close you and your family are to Mrs. Kopek," Mr. Findley said. "You'll be pretty torn up about what we've got to tell you."

I stepped out from beside the stove. "Mrs. Kopek?" I cried. "Has something happened to her?"

"Yes," Mr. Povich said, not looking at me, still talking to Papa. "There was a trail of blood from Findley's place over to old Mrs. Kopek's. We followed it right up to her front porch. The snow was trampled and bloody, and there were scratches all over the door."

"Dear God!" Papa said. "Did they get in?"

"No, but they finished her off, anyway."

"What do you mean?"

"Looks like she had a heart attack. We saw a lamp shining in the hall, so we broke in when she didn't come to the door. There she was, in her robe and slippers, a rifle on the floor beside her. The poor old lady must have died of fright."

I ran over to Papa, crying, and he quickly set his rifle down and put his arms around me. My heart was doing peculiar things, pounding and leaping around in my chest, and I was trembling all over.

"Papa," I sobbed, "she's dead. Mrs. Kopek's dead!"

Papa's arms tightened around me, rocking me slightly, keeping me safe. "Therese, Therese. Please don't cry," he said helplessly. "Mrs. Kopek was old, and she always said she wanted to go quickly when her time came."

"But not like that," I protested. "Not with a wolf

trying to get in at her. She must have been so scared. And she was all alone, too!"

Papa cleared his throat a couple of times. Finally he said, "She didn't feel any pain, Therese. Her heart stopped, that's all. We've got to remember that she went fast and felt no pain."

I pressed my face against Papa and wept silently, my hot tears soaking into the rough wool of his jacket. I didn't care if the men were watching me or not.

There was an awkward silence, then Mr. Povich continued, gruffly but gently. "We covered Mrs. Kopek with an afghan. It was the best we could do for now. Our wives will go over in the morning and prepare her for burial."

One of the Lindstrom boys who had come into the kitchen with Mr. Povich spoke up. "We followed the wolf's tracks in the snow out to your west pasture. That's where they disappeared. That wolf ought to be around here somewhere."

Papa shook his head. "I haven't heard anything. Surely my livestock would have roused me if there was a pack of wolves running loose on my land."

"Not a pack," Mr. Povich said. "Just one. The white wolf. The others seemed to disappear into thin air, but the tracks we followed were large and speckled with blood. It's the white one we're trying to hunt down."

"I'm coming, too."

I raised my head to see what was happening.

Pinky had entered the kitchen. He stood there, fully dressed, fur hat in one hand, rifle in the other.

"I'm coming, too," he repeated.

"No, Pinky," Papa said. "You'd better stay here. If that wolf tried to get into Mrs. Kopek's house, it might . . ."

"That's right," Mr. Povich put in. "There's a woman and her children here. Someone ought to stay and protect them."

The men nodded their approval. They clattered out into the yard and picked up their torches. I heard them stamping their feet and muttering to each other while they waited for Papa to saddle his horse and join them. Finally the group rode off.

Pinky went to the door and fastened it securely.

"Pinky," I said. "Will it be all right?"

"I don't know, Therese," he replied. "I don't know."

Just then a faint, weak voice called to us from across the hall, from the parlor, the room we never used, except on Sundays when the priest came to visit.

"Pinky? Therese?"

It was Mama.

Pinky picked up the lamp. "Is that you, Madam?" he asked.

We hurried into the parlor.

Mama was sitting on the horsehair settee, cradling her arm and rocking back and forth as if in pain.

"I don't know what happened," she said. "I've been in a faint. I must have fallen down the stairs and hurt myself. My arm's bleeding, and I think the bone is broken."

EIGHT

▪ Mama ▪

Mama!

Mama was hurt. Mama needed me. Everything else had to wait.

Pinky and I managed to get her upstairs and into bed. Mama was in such pain that she fainted once, and Pinky and I actually had to carry her between us.

Her side of the bed was rumpled, and the quilt was thrown halfway up over the pillow. It looked like someone was sleeping in the bed. Papa must not have noticed she was gone when he got up and ran downstairs to the door.

Pinky sent me to the kitchen for a kettle of hot water so he could examine the wound. Somehow, with only one hand, Mama had managed to tear a strip from the bottom of her nightgown and wrap it around her arm. The flannel was bloody and sticking to the wound in places. Pinky would have to sponge it with water in order to get it loose without hurting her.

I had to get the stove going again, feeding it newspaper and bits of kindling before I could start a good blaze. Then the kettle of water seemed to take forever to heat. When it finally began whistling, I grabbed a basin, wrapped a tea towel around the handle of the kettle so I could carry it comfortably, and hurried upstairs.

Mama opened her eyes and looked at me lovingly as I came into the room. Pinky had propped her up on pillows and covered her with the quilt.

"What a good girl you are, Therese," she said softly. "Where's Joey? I don't want him to see me like this. It might frighten him."

"He's fast asleep, Mama," I reassured her. "I didn't hear a sound when I passed his door. He's just like Papa. He sleeps like a dead man."

"Papa?" For the first time since we'd found her in the parlor, Mama seemed to realize that Papa was missing. "Where is he? Is he out in the barn?"

Pinky and I exchanged startled glances. Hadn't she heard Mr. Povich's loud knocking and all the talk in the kitchen?

"No, Mama," I told her. "It's after two o'clock in the morning. Papa's ridden off with a hunting party. The wolves got into Mr. Findley's barn and killed one of his horses."

"Wolves?" A dazed, puzzled expression clouded her grey eyes. "Oh, yes. They are out there, aren't they? I thought I was only dreaming. . . ."

Pinky poured some water into the basin, wet the tea towel, and began to dab at the makeshift bandage, loosening it and finally unwrapping it. He drew in his breath sharply when he saw what it covered.

Between Mama's elbow and shoulder ran a long, jagged wound. Pinky gently prodded the skin surrounding it.

"I don't think the bone's been broken," he said, "but it's a deep gash. Therese, bring me a piece of clean cloth to bind it up again."

I went down the hall to the linen closet and found an old but clean pillowcase. I didn't want to use one of the new ones. Mama had worked so hard on them, crocheting lace all around the hems.

I ran back into the bedroom and handed Pinky the pillowcase. He put one end in his teeth and tore off several long strips.

I saw him press the ragged lips of the wound together and wrap the cloth about it, working quickly and expertly. It had begun to bleed heavily again.

Mama moaned softly as he ripped more strips from what was left of the pillowcase and tied them around her arm.

"This will have to do for now," he told her. "I'll go quickly and get Dr. McNally."

"Wait!" Mama reached out with her good arm and clutched Pinky's hand. "Don't go yet. Can you tell me, Pinky, what happened to me? Why was I in the parlor? How did I hurt myself?"

"Can't you remember anything? Anything at all?" he asked.

"Yes, but they were strange things. Unbeliev-able things," Mama said, groaning. "Oh, my arm hurts so badly. Do I have a fever, Therese? Per-haps I have been hallucinating."

I laid my hand gently on her forehead. It was cool. Too cool. "No, Mama. You don't have a fever."

"What sort of strange things do you remember?" Pinky asked softly, urgently. His face was pale.

Mama drew a ragged breath and looked away. Then she closed her eyes and frowned, concen-trating on what Pinky had asked her to remember.

"I must have been dreaming. That's the only explanation. I fell and hurt myself. Then I fainted, and the pain made me dream those awful dreams."

"Can you describe them?" Pinky asked, leaning closer to her.

"Yes. I was in such terrible pain. My arm was bleeding, and I was all alone out in the snow. There had been others with me, I think, but now they were gone. I found myself running desperately toward Mrs. Kopek's house. Surely she will help me, I thought. Dear, kind Mrs. Kopek."

Pinky's body tensed. He slipped his hand from Mama's grasp in one quick motion and took a step backward, away from the bed.

"Just a moment, Madam," he said in an odd, tight voice. "Therese, why don't you look in on Joey? He might be awake and frightened."

"He's fine, Pinky," I said, impatient to hear Mama's story. "If Joey were awake, he'd be out here."

"Then why don't you go down to the kitchen and fix your mother a cup of tea?"

"I will," I said. "But first I want to hear what Mama has to say."

I used a firm tone of voice with Pinky when I said that, so he'd know I meant business. For some reason he was trying to get rid of me. But I wasn't leaving, not this time. My place was with Mama.

Mama started to talk again, anyway.

"I stumbled up on Mrs. Kopek's porch," she continued, "and began to hammer on her door. No, it was more as if I were scratching at the door. Oh, everything is so confused."

"Mama, oh Mama," I said, tears beginning to

form in my eyes again. "How strange you should have dreamed about Mrs. Kopek when—"

Pinky silenced me by raising his hand. I realized he was right. Mama didn't need to hear the bad news yet.

Mama kept talking. "Finally, through the window in the door, I saw a light approaching. And then Mrs. Kopek looked out. 'Mrs. Kopek! Mrs. Kopek!' I cried. 'Help me!' But the words didn't come out right. They didn't sound like words at all."

I noticed that Pinky was trembling now. It wasn't like him to be so nervous, but then Mama's arm had really looked bad, and her suffering must have upset him.

"Go on," he urged.

Mama gritted her teeth, as if the pain of her arm was too much to endure, but she went on.

"Mrs. Kopek stared at me, as if I were an evil spirit. Her eyes widened in terror. Then she began to scream. 'Please, Mrs. Kopek,' I begged. 'I need your help!' But she continued to scream. And then the screaming stopped. I heard her fall to the floor.

I waited, but I couldn't hear her moving about. Then the next thing I knew, I was here in the parlor."

Again I thought how strange it was that Mama dreamed of Mrs. Kopek at the very time when . . . But Mama had done that before. Sometimes she would have funny, cloudy dreams that came true later. Mrs. Kopek used to say she knew a lot of women who could do that back in Russia.

Now Mama struggled to rise up from her pillow, but I put my hand gently on her good shoulder to stop her.

"Please, Mama, you have to lie back and rest. You mustn't get upset over those crazy dreams."

"But they seemed so real," she insisted.

"Nightmares always seem real," I said. "Mine do." I hoped she wouldn't try to get up again. The effort had made her lips turn white, and her face looked haggard and pinched.

"Pinky!" I cried. "We're wasting time. Go for the doctor. Can't you see that Mama is suffering?"

I followed him out into the hall.

"I'll take good care of Mama while you're gone," I promised. "But hurry! Please hurry!"

Pinky looked down into my upturned face and slowly removed his Saint Mikhail medal. Then he kissed it and placed it over my head.

"Wear this," he told me. "It will keep you safe."

I started to tell him that he was being silly—what danger was I in? But he ran down the stairs to the kitchen. I heard him rummaging for his coat and boots. Then he was gone.

I went back into Mama's room and sat down beside her. Her face was as white as the pillow she rested on, and her eyes were closed.

When Papa comes home, I thought, he'll make things right. Papa is clever and good. He'll make Mama well again.

Mama opened her eyes and gave me a hint of a smile.

"But do you know what, Therese? When Mrs. Kopek was screaming, I saw that she was not wearing her false teeth. Isn't it odd, the things you dream?"

▪When▪Papa▪ Came▪

At dawn, Papa, Pinky, and Dr. McNally all arrived together.

First there were voices in the kitchen, then foot-steps on the stairs.

I got up slowly from the chair I'd been sitting in at Mama's bedside. My legs were cramped and stiff from having been tucked beneath me. Little needles of pain shot through them, and I shook and stamped them as quietly as I could so as not to disturb Mama.

Mama opened her eyes when Papa and the doctor entered the room.

Dr. McNally laid his black bag on the night-stand and stood looking down on her as Papa went to the other side of the bed and took her good hand.

"Are you all right, darling?" Papa asked anx-iously. "Pinky says your arm is pretty cut up."

"What a clumsy wife you have, Anthony," Mama said, trying to smile while she struggled erect on her pillow. I saw her wince and bite her lips as a fresh stain reddened the bandages. "I must have fallen down the stairs in the dark, and I've hurt myself quite badly, I'm afraid."

"Well, let's take a look at what we've got here," the doctor said. "Maybe it isn't as serious as Pinky thinks it is."

He carefully unwrapped the strips of cloth that bound Mama's arm and whistled in amazement when he saw the wound.

"You did all this in a fall?" he asked, adjusting his spectacles for a closer inspection. "I'd say it looks more like a bullet wound. See? As if a bullet plowed its way upward, opening the flesh, and then exited the wound here."

"Nonsense, Doctor," Papa said impatiently. "My

wife certainly would know if she'd been shot, wouldn't she? Besides, she hasn't left the house."

Dr. McNally didn't reply. He pursed his mouth, squinted, and continued to poke and prod at Mama's arm.

"Well, how she managed to do all this to herself in a fall is beyond me, but that's not important at the moment," he finally said. "Fortunately, she did no damage to the bone. First I must clean the wound, and then I'm afraid I will have to do some pretty fancy suturing."

Suturing? Did he mean *sewing*? The thought of Dr. McNally stitching up Mama's slender, white arm with a needle and thread made my toes curl and my stomach roll over.

I must have made some sound, because my father looked over and seemed to notice me for the first time since he'd come into the room.

"Therese? Oh, my poor little Therese. You've been taking care of Mama for me, haven't you?"

I nodded, trying not to cry.

Papa put his arms around me and led me to the door.

"You mustn't worry. Everything will be all right now," he told me. "The doctor will take care of Mama's arm, and she'll be fine, just fine."

"But Papa," I said, twisting in his arms and trying to look back into the bedroom. "He said he had to sew up Mama's arm."

"Yes," Papa told me. "It will hurt Mama a little, and I think she'd prefer you didn't watch. But when he's finished, her arm won't bleed anymore, and it will begin to heal."

He bent down and kissed my cheek. "Pinky said you helped him carry Mama upstairs and took care of her when he went for the doctor. Is that right?"

I nodded again.

"I've always known I could count on you in an emergency, Therese," he said with a smile. "I'm very proud of you for what you did last night, and I know Mama is, too."

I felt at least two inches taller when he said that. It was true—I had taken good care of Mama last night, hadn't I?

Then he looked toward Joey's room and said,

"Your brother will be waking up soon, Therese. It would be a big help if you would take him down to the kitchen and fix his breakfast. Do you think you can cook his porridge and see to it he doesn't bother Mama?"

"Of course, Papa. I've done it before."

"That's my girl." Papa patted my shoulder and hurried back to Mama's bedside.

Right then, Joey appeared in his doorway, yawning and scratching his plump little middle. He looked like a pouter pigeon in his robe and pajamas.

"Good morning, Therese," he said cheerfully. "I'm hungry. Are you?"

"Listen, Joey," I said. "Mama's not feeling well this morning."

"Mama's sick? May I go see her?"

"No, not now. Maybe later. Papa says you must be very quiet and not bother Mama, and that I'm to fix your breakfast."

"Really?" Joey thought for a moment and then said, "Will you make me toast fingers, Therese? With jam? I'll be very quiet if you make me toast fingers."

"No, you're supposed to have porridge."

Joey set his jaw in a way that reminded me of Papa. "I don't want porridge. I want toast fingers."

He sat at the table and watched while I sliced bread into fingers and fried them in hot bacon fat. When they puffed a little and turned crisp and brown, I removed them from the pan and spread them with cherry jam. Then I added a large dollop of tinned baked beans, Joey's favorite, and placed the plate before him. He tucked into it with relish, and I left in search of Pinky.

Pinky was just outside the back door, tinkering with the pump.

"The doctor is taking stitches in Mama's arm," I told him. "Do you think it hurts a lot when he does that?"

I couldn't see Pinky's eyes, because he was wearing his smoked glasses. I did see him frown, though.

"You shouldn't be out here, Therese, in your robe and slippers. We don't want the doctor treating you for pneumonia, do we?"

As I pulled my woolen robe closer about me, I

felt Pinky's silver medal around my neck. I had forgotten about it.

"Here's your Saint Mikhail medal, Pinky," I said, removing it and holding it out to him. "Why did you think I needed it last night?"

Pinky laid down his wrench and took the medal from me, looking down at it for a moment before he kissed it and placed it over his head.

"Why, Pinky?" I persisted.

"Because of the wolves," he said reluctantly. "But you are safe now, at least for the moment."

"What about the wolves? Didn't Papa and the others find them last night?"

"No. They disappeared. The white one, too."

"Do you think they'll come again?"

"Yes. I'm sure they are still with us."

"I hope not," I said. "Their howling makes Mama act so strangely."

I felt Pinky's stare from behind his dark glasses.

"And what do you know, Therese, about your mother's behavior when the wolves howl? Did you—"

"I hear Papa and the doctor in the kitchen," I

broke in. "The doctor must have finished treating Mama. I want to hear how she is."

I returned to the house, glad to leave Pinky behind, since he seemed to be in another one of his moods.

"I've given her something to make her sleep," Dr. McNally was saying. "I'm afraid, though, that she will always have a long and rather unpleasant-looking scar on her arm."

Joey was still at the table, his mouth smeared with jam. "Did Mama hurt her arm?" he asked. "Is it as bad as when I skinned my elbow last summer?"

"Worse, I'm afraid," Papa said, wetting a napkin and wiping Joey's face. "Oh, there you are, Therese. Would you please take Joey upstairs and let him see Mama? She was asking for him."

"You must be very quiet," I told Joey before I allowed him into Mama's bedroom. "She's sleepy, and you mustn't talk loudly or bounce on her bed."

"I *know*," Joey said indignantly. "I remember how

I felt when I hurt my elbow. I was afraid somebody would bump it."

He tiptoed into the room and hovered anxiously over Mama's bed. Mama opened her eyes and smiled up at him.

"Poor Mama," he said in what he obviously thought was a grown-up voice. "Would it make your arm better if I kissed it?"

"Yes, darling. I'm sure it would."

Mama smiled as he bent over and kissed her arm. "Oh, thank you, Joey. That *did* make it feel better."

"Therese made me fried toast fingers for breakfast," Joey told her. "They were good—but not as good as yours, of course," he amended hastily, afraid of hurting her feelings.

Mama laughed. Her eyes were full of love as she looked at me.

"What would I do without you, Therese? You sat beside me all night, didn't you? Every time I woke up, I saw you there in the chair. I'm very fortunate to have such a kind, thoughtful daughter."

"And me. What about me?" demanded Joey. "I'm the one who made your arm all better by kissing it."

Mama rumpled his hair with her good hand.

"No one's ever likely to forget you, Joey," she said. "Perhaps you'll be a doctor someday. You won't need a black bag, as Dr. McNally does. All you'll have to do is kiss people to make them well."

Joey darted from the room and returned with his favorite book. He wriggled himself into the bedside chair and opened the book.

"You don't need to stay, Therese," he said importantly. "I'll read to Mama until she falls asleep."

Joey's idea of "reading" was to look at the pictures and tell the story. I looked at Mama hesitantly, but she smiled and nodded.

"All right, Joey, but do it softly," I cautioned. Then I blew Mama a kiss and left the room.

I glanced out the hall window to see if Dr. McNally had left. His sleigh was no longer in the yard.

Papa and Pinky were talking as I started downstairs. I paused and sat down on one of the steps to adjust my bedroom slipper, but the anger in Papa's voice startled me, and I sat, frozen, one hand on my foot as I listened to what they were saying.

It's true what they say about eavesdropping. You never hear anything good. What Papa and Pinky said to each other that morning will haunt me all the days of my life.

TEN

·Pinky·

Have you gone completely mad, Pinky?" Papa was demanding in a low, harsh voice. "What kind of story are you making up now? What's this non-sense about my wife and the wolves?"

"I wish to God it was just a story," Pinky said. "But you must listen to me. I don't know how to tell you this, but I must. I know I'm making a bad job of it."

"Yes, you are."

"Let me try again, then," Pinky said.

I could hear him take a deep breath.

"Things have been happening in this house," he said. "To Madam. It all began when the wolves first came down from the north. I have tried to deny my suspicions, to make up explanations for the things I have seen. But now there is this— what happened last night with Madam and the white wolf."

"You're still not making any sense," Papa said. "What suspicions? What have you seen?"

"Don't you see? The wounds match. The white wolf was shot in the front leg and your wife has a bullet wound in her arm."

"Am I losing my mind, too? I can't follow you, Pinky. What does one thing have to do with the other? And besides, my wife's injury is not a bullet wound. How many times do I have to say that? She fell down the stairs. That's how she hurt herself. It's as simple as that."

"But the doctor said it looked like a bullet wound," Pinky said. "I was listening. I heard."

"Dr. McNally's an old man. He makes mistakes. And do you really expect me to believe my wife has some connection with the white wolf because she hurt her arm the same night he got shot in the leg?"

"Yes. I told you what Madam said last night. She said she dreamed she ran up on Mrs. Kopek's porch and scratched at the door. *Scratched*. Those were her words. Then she described how she peered in through the window, and how Mrs. Kopek, seeing her, screamed with fear and fell to the floor. And didn't Mr. Povich say they found the bloody footprints of the white wolf on the porch, and claw marks on the door? And didn't poor Mrs. Kopek die of shock and fright, her rifle by her side?"

Pinky paused for a moment, then said, "So tell me, how would Madam have known all that if she hadn't seen it with her own eyes?"

"Her own eyes? There is no way my wife could have been at Mrs. Kopek's last night," Papa said.

"Then how could she describe everything exactly as it happened?"

"My God, Pinky! What is all this? The explanation is perfectly simple."

"Then tell it to me, please," Pinky begged, "so I can believe it, too."

"All right. My wife knew all the facts of Mrs. Kopek's death because she overheard what Mr. Povich said last night in the kitchen," Papa said.

A chair creaked, and I heard someone's foot scrape against the floor.

"Try to imagine what happened," Papa continued. "She'd gotten up at some time during the night and had fallen down the stairs and hurt her arm. So she dragged herself into the parlor and lost consciousness. Then Povich came, and while she was drifting in and out of this . . . this swoon, or whatever it was, she heard him talking about the white wolf and Mrs. Kopek, and she incorporated it into her dreams."

"So how do you explain the fact that she'd been outside, last night, running in the snow?"

"What are you talking about, Pinky? She didn't go outside at any time last night."

"She'd been outside," Pinky insisted. "I saw her feet."

"Her feet? What about her feet?"

"When she was in the parlor. I saw her feet. They were blue with cold, and they were scraped and bruised. I treated them later, when Therese was out of the room. I didn't want her to see and ask questions."

A silence. A long silence. Then Papa's voice:

"I'm trying to understand exactly what it is you're trying to tell me, Pinky."

"That your wife was out running in the snow last night. So were the wolves," Pinky began.

"And?" asked Papa.

"She was barefoot. In the snow. And it wasn't just last night, either. I stopped her from going out another time, when the wolves were howling. She has gone out many more nights since then I'm sure of it now."

"And just what makes you so sure?"

"From the way she's been acting. Surely you've noticed how oddly she's been behaving lately, and that it happens when the moon is full and the wolves are out. Then, tonight, when the white wolf received a bullet wound—"

"So get to the point, Pinky," Papa snapped. "I

think I see where you're headed, God forgive you, but I want you to come flat out and say it, so you can hear how crazy it sounds. Come on, Pinky. Say it!"

"Must I say it? Must I put it into words?" Pinky's voice was sad. "You were there, thirteen years ago, when she came to the Kopeks' door, half frozen, not knowing who she was or where she came from, with her feet cut and bleeding!"

Papa didn't answer.

"At that time, too, the wolves were down from the north," Pinky continued.

He paused for a moment and then finally spoke in a low, pitying voice. "And you've suspected, all these years, that there was something terribly wrong, something unnatural about your wife, haven't you?"

I sat there on the stairs, gnawing at my bottom lip, wondering what to do. What to think.

Mama, I thought. What are they saying about Mama? It was like a nightmare.

Then the nightmare got worse.

I heard Pinky say, "Listen to me. Please listen to me. Can't you see how hard it is for me to say what I am saying? That, unknown to herself, these past weeks your wife has been assuming the shape and nature of a wolf?"

"You've always claimed to be an expert on wolves, haven't you, Pinky?" Papa asked bitterly, after a terrible moment of silence.

There was a pleading note in Pinky's voice when he replied, "Don't mock me. I'm only thinking of the children. What if she gets worse? What if she attacks the children?"

Up there in that cold stairwell, I closed my eyes and shuddered. Attack us? What does Pinky mean? Mama would never do anything like that. She'd never once, as far back as I could remember, spanked either Joey or me, even when we'd been naughty.

"There was a wolf woman in a neighboring village, back in Russia," Pinky was saying. "It killed its human children."

Papa spoke quietly and evenly, but his voice was tinged with desperation. "You're mad, Pinky.

You've gone mad. Or maybe you've been mad all along, and I didn't know it."

"Yes, I realize it must seem that way," Pinky replied, "but—"

"Don't say another word," my father interrupted. "I can't stand the sound of your voice. I want you off my property as soon as possible. I'll give you two months' wages and one of the horses. Then I never want to see you or hear from you again."

"I can understand why you must send me away. But the children! What will happen to the children?" Pinky asked. "She will harm the children!"

"You leave my children out of this craziness. You are not to speak to them before you go. I've given you my ultimatum. Pack up and get out, or I'll call the law on you, Pinky."

I could hear the tears in Pinky's voice when he asked, "Will tomorrow be soon enough? There are some things I must do first."

"Yes. Early tomorrow will be fine—before Therese and Joey wake up. But I want you to take your belongings and sleep in the bunkhouse tonight," Papa said. "And I don't want you working for any of my neighbors, either. I won't have you spreading your sick stories about my wife."

Pinky didn't answer at first. Then he cleared his throat and said in a stricken voice, "You—your wife and children—they have always meant everything to me. You are my family. I would never do anything to harm you."

"I always assumed you felt that way, Pinky," Papa said. "And surely you must know that we've all felt the same way about you."

Papa seemed to pause. One of the two men blew his nose loudly. "The children . . . why, the children think of you as . . . But how can I have you here, working alongside me and playing with Therese and Joey, with you believing that my wife is a . . . a . . ."

"A lycanthrope? A wolf woman?"

There was a terrible sadness in Pinky's voice when he said that. "But she is, you know. There are such things. They have been with us for many centuries. I don't know how they came to be, but they are real."

He took a deep breath and said calmly, "Your wife came into your life thirteen years ago, the year the wolves came. And she will leave you now, with the wolves, her animal nature strengthened and more dangerous. I only pray she won't—"

"No, not that again!" Papa burst out. "You *are* mad, Pinky—stark, raving mad. It's best you leave now."

I couldn't stand to hear anymore. I put my hands over my ears and ran up the stairs to my room.

ELEVEN

·Therese· and · Pinky·

I flung myself on my bed.

What was happening? I asked myself. What was Pinky saying about Mama? And what had he called her? A wolf woman?

Wolf. Why did Pinky think Mama was able to turn herself into a wolf? Whoever heard of such a thing?

And he kept talking about Mama hurting us. Mama? One thing I knew, one thing I was sure of, was that Mama, dear, gentle Mama, would never hurt anyone, and certainly not Papa, Joey, or me.

Papa said Pinky had gone mad. Insane. Was that it? Had Pinky lost his mind? *Our* Pinky? Yes, that had to be it. That's the only reason Pinky would ever say terrible things like that about Mama. Pinky had always been so fond of Mama.

Papa once told me about people who went insane. He explained what happened, and what it was like for them. He said it was like getting sick. They couldn't help what happened to them, any more than a person can help getting the flu or the measles. He said insanity was a sickness of the mind, and that we should be kind and understanding to people like that. He said most people didn't understand that, though.

So why was Papa getting angry at Pinky, when he knew about insane people? Maybe it was because Pinky had said those awful things about Mama, and Papa forgot to be kind and understanding, because he felt Pinky was hurting Mama with his words.

Yes. That must be it. It had to be.

Maybe I should be angry at Pinky, too, the way

Papa was. And yet, Pinky seemed so sad. I felt sorry for him. I couldn't help feeling more sorry than angry. Sorry for Pinky for losing his mind, and sorry for us—all of us—because if Pinky left, nothing would ever be the same again.

Pinky had been with us for as far back as I could remember. It had always been Papa and Mama and Joey and me and Pinky. The five of us. We'd been a family.

I remembered Pinky teaching me to ride a horse. And telling me how pretty I was, when a girl at school called me an ugly old troll. And, at Christmas, watching me when I unwrapped his present. He liked making presents for Joey and me. He'd carve little animals out of wood—fat little squirrels and cats and pigs—and he'd make me cornhusk dolls with acorns for hats.

I loved Pinky. I would miss him when he left.

Maybe I should go to him and tell him so, I thought. Maybe it would make him better. Maybe he wouldn't be sad if I told him I loved him.

I got up from the bed and realized I was still

in my robe and nightgown. My clothes seemed to tie themselves in knots as I put them on.

When I'd finally managed to dress myself, I looked in on Mama. She was fast asleep, her bandaged arm resting on top of the quilt. Joey was curled up in a chair, sleeping too. He must have read them both to sleep.

Then I went down to the storeroom. Pinky's things were gone. It hadn't taken him long to move back to the bunkhouse.

I lifted Mama's shawl down off the peg by the door and wrapped myself in it. It was so long that it hung down to my ankles. Pulling it closely about me, I made my way carefully over the frozen snow.

Papa was in the barn, working. I could hear his voice, soothing the horses.

I went past as quickly as I could on the slippery ground. I didn't want Papa to know I was going to talk to Pinky. It might get Pinky into even more trouble.

Reaching the bunkhouse, I put my ear to the door and listened. Yes, Pinky was in there. I heard him moving about.

I knocked once, then twice. When Pinky didn't answer, I pushed the door open and went in.

He was standing at the potbellied stove, so intent on what he was doing that he didn't hear me enter. The stove was red hot, and a small hand bellows lay on the floor.

He was melting something in a small iron pot —something the color of silver. The pot had a pouring spout on it.

I glanced quickly at his neck. Pinky's medal and chain were missing.

Then I saw him pour the liquid silver into a bullet mold. Pinky was making bullets. No, just one bullet.

"Pinky," I said, "why are you making a bullet from your Saint Mikhail medal?"

Pinky started so violently that a few drops of the silver spilled out on the stove.

"Therese! I didn't hear you come in."

"But why, Pinky?" I repeated. "That's the medal you wear to protect yourself from the Dark One."

Pinky looked at me for a few moments before replying.

"Perhaps there is no Dark One, Therese. Only sad, lonely ones," he said slowly.

"But will you wear the bullet around your neck?" I persisted.

"No," he said. I'd never seen Pinky look as unhappy as he did at that moment. "I shall put it in a rifle."

"I don't understand."

"Just understand this, Therese: If I use this bullet, I am only doing it out of love for you and your family."

"Why, Pinky," I said delightedly, figuring this was the perfect time to tell him why I'd come. "That's exactly what I've been wanting to tell you! That I love you, too, I mean."

I hurried on, confident that he couldn't possibly guess I knew he was leaving. "I was just thinking that if you ever had to leave us for any reason— and I can't imagine what it might be—that, well, I didn't want you to go without knowing I love you, Pinky. I always will."

Pinky's pale eyes were misty, but his lips were smiling, as though I'd said something that amused him.

"Oh, Therese," he said. "My dear, funny little Therese. I love you, too."

He went to the stove and turned his back to me.

As I left the bunkhouse, I noticed that his shoulders were shaking.

At the time, I thought he was laughing.

I realize now that Pinky was crying.

TWELVE

▪The▪Last▪Night▪

Papa cooked supper that night. He fried ham and eggs, the only meal he knew how to cook.

"Where's Pinky?" Joey asked, looking up from his plate. "Why isn't he eating with us?"

"He's moved back to the bunkhouse," Papa said shortly.

"Well, I miss him," Joey said. "Especially with Mama not here."

I'd taken some tea and toast upstairs to Mama earlier. She hadn't seemed hungry, but I stayed and made her finish it.

I watched her while she ate, her silver-gilt hair spilling down her back. She looked so beautiful. She smiled at me over the toast, telling me I had fixed it just the way she liked it.

How could Pinky possibly think she was a—whatever it was he called her? I asked myself. Yes, without a doubt, Pinky was mad. That was the only possible explanation for the terrible things he had said.

I hoped he'd be able to find another job somewhere and manage to hide the fact that he wasn't quite right in the head. Maybe he'd get better in time. And then, perhaps, he'd come back to us.

I was clearing the table in the kitchen when we heard horses in the yard and a banging at the door. My stomach lurched at the sound. I used to look forward to callers. Now they usually meant trouble.

It was Mr. Povich and his hunting party.

"Get your gun," he shouted at Papa. "The wolves are out again. They've been sighted a couple of miles from here. The white wolf isn't with them, though. It's probably gone to ground somewhere and is licking its wounds, thanks to Findley and his rifle. If we hurry, we might be able to get the whole bunch."

"Lock the door behind me, Therese," Papa said when he left. "And don't go outside for any reason. I don't know when I'll be home."

I obeyed Papa, bolting the door as he stomped out in his boots to join the others. I washed and dried the supper dishes and put Joey to bed. Then I looked in on Mama. She was sleeping, but she tossed and turned restlessly. I wondered if she had a fever. I didn't go in and feel her forehead, though, in case I might disturb her.

Finally I put a lamp in the kitchen window for Papa and went to bed.

It had been a long, worrisome day, full of events I preferred not to think about, so I fell asleep almost immediately.

I suddenly woke up and sat bolt upright in my bed. The full moon was shining in my window, lighting up every corner of the room.

Something is wrong, I thought, breaking into a cold sweat. *Something is happening out there!*

It was almost as though someone had nudged me in the ribs and whispered the words.

I grabbed my robe, thrust my feet into my slippers, and ran down the stairs.

The lamp was still burning in the window, but a cold wind was blowing through the kitchen. The door wasn't locked. It stood ajar, creaking back and forth on its hinges.

Someone had come in! I shook my head, trying to clear my thoughts. No—no. The latch was on the inside of the door. Someone had gone *out!*

I remembered the time Mama had been sleepwalking and tried to open the door. And then I remembered what Pinky had said to Papa, about Mama and the wolves. And suddenly it didn't seem so crazy anymore.

Mama! Mama had gone out to join the wolves!

I started for the storeroom. Then I realized Pinky wasn't there. He was in the bunkhouse. I would have to go to the bunkhouse and find him. He would know what to do.

I ran through the door and out into the yard. The snow that covered the ground was icy, frozen.

I felt the bitter cold through the thin soles of my slippers, yet I hurried on.

What if Pinky was out with the hunters? Or what if he'd packed up and left already?

"Oh Pinky, please be there!" I was sobbing now. I had to find Mama soon, or something terrible would happen. I knew it. I could feel it.

The moon lit up the yard. Snowdrifts cast evil shadows, like crouching gnomes, on the ground.

My teeth were chattering, more from fear than cold, and I clenched my jaws as I ran toward the bunkhouse.

And then it happened—the unspeakable thing I have tried and tried to forget.

I heard the jingle of horses' bridles, and the sound of men shouting.

Around the corner of the barn, straight toward me, ran the white wolf.

It was running clumsily on three legs. Its other one had some sort of bloody bandage on it. I remember standing there, wondering stupidly how a wolf could bandage its own leg.

"Therese! Therese! Run back to the house! Quickly!"

It was Papa. He appeared seemingly out of nowhere, leading the hunting party. He leapt off his horse and ran toward me, raising his rifle and pointing it at the wolf.

"Get out of the way, Therese, so I can shoot!"

I stood where I was, as if turned to stone.

The wolf was only a few yards away now, and drawing closer. It was panting from exhaustion, and its tongue lolled from its mouth, red and dripping. But its eyes—its lovely, silvery grey eyes—looked at me, not as though it wished to do me harm, but in a mute appeal for help.

It stopped running—sliding and almost falling on the frozen snow. Then it righted itself and advanced toward me slowly, crouching down on its front legs, head lowered, the way dogs do when they want to let you know they're friendly and won't bite.

"Move away!" Papa's voice was more of a sob than a shout.

I saw him sight down the barrel of the rifle.

"Listen to me, Therese!" he called. "Back away

slowly. Don't make any sudden moves. It's too late to run now. It's too close."

"No, wait! It won't hurt me, Papa—" I started to say.

But then I heard the crack of a rifle. It was a sharp, clear sound, and it came from somewhere on my right.

The wolf fell to the ground, writhing. Then it lay still.

Pinky strode silently from the shadows, his rifle smoking. He came over to me and knelt beside the wolf. Tears were streaming down his cheeks.

"You killed it, Pinky!" I cried. "You killed it, and it was so beautiful!"

I threw myself down on my knees in the snow, next to the lovely, dying creature. I put my hand on its head. Its fur felt like warm silk beneath my hand. Its eyes were closed, but it was still breathing, its flanks going out and in, fighting for every breath.

Papa and the others ran across the yard. "Thank God you're safe, Therese," he said, kneeling beside me and pressing me to his chest.

I struggled free, pushing his arms away roughly.

"But it wasn't going to hurt me! I tried to tell you that, but you wouldn't listen!"

Pinky stared at me. In the moonlight his pale eyes looked blind. Lost.

"No! Don't say that, Therese!" he begged. "She *was* going to hurt you. I was sure she was. She was going straight for you!"

"*She?*" Mr. Povich said, drawing closer to the wolf. "*She?* Whoever heard of a she-wolf leading a pack?"

He picked up one of the wolf's hind legs, peered at its underbelly, then dropped the leg carelessly. At that moment, I hated him more than anything in the world.

"Well, darned if you aren't right, Pinky. It *was* a she-wolf."

The wolf twitched feebly. It opened its lovely eyes and looked at me—such sad, beautiful eyes. I wondered if it knew it was dying.

Please God, don't let it know it's dying, I thought.

The members of the hunting party pressed in closer, congratulating themselves on the fact that at last they'd caught the white wolf.

I hated them. I hated them all.

And I hated Pinky. Pinky, the wolf killer. I hated him almost as much as I hated Mr. Povich.

"Why, Pinky?" I sobbed. "Why?"

Pinky threw his rifle to the ground, pushing it roughly and angrily away from him. It slid across the ice with a curious rattling sound.

Then he laid his hands on the head of the wolf, reverently, as if he were blessing it.

And then, to everyone's amazement, he said what sounded like a funeral prayer.

Pinky said, "Go forth, O unhappy spirit, from this troubled body and imperfect world into the paradise that has been prepared for you by the Almighty Father. . . ."

I couldn't understand anything that was happening. I let Papa put his arms around me again and buried my face in his jacket.

"My God—look!"

Mr. Povich's voice was shrill with hysteria. "Oh, my God! My God!"

I can hardly put into words what happened next, even though I relive it every night now, in my nightmares.

Papa's body began to tremble convulsively. He grasped my head with his hands and pressed it hard against him, so that I couldn't turn and see. Then he began to make a strange, whimpering sound deep in his throat, like an animal.

His arms suddenly slackened and went limp, falling to his sides. I pulled away from him and looked up at his face.

His mouth was trembling, and he was staring down over my head at the wolf.

Only it wasn't the white wolf who was lying there now. It was Mama.

Yes, it was Mama who lay there, pale and still, in her white nightgown with a red splash down the front.

She fixed her eyes on Pinky—those silvery grey eyes. Why hadn't I recognized them? And she said, "You knew, didn't you, Pinky, even before I did?"

Pinky's voice was broken and uneven. "I had to do it," he said, "for your husband, for your children."

"Yes," Mama said. A little bubble of blood pulsed

at the corner of her mouth. "It would have come to that in the end. I would have harmed Anthony and the children."

Her breathing was labored. She gathered her strength and said, each word coming painfully, "Listen to me, Pinky. You must never regret what you did. It was the only way. I understand everything now, and you did the only thing a true friend could do."

Then she turned her head and looked, first at Papa, then at me. Her lips moved. She was trying to say something. I think she was trying to comfort us, but her life was fleeing fast, and in the end she could only sigh.

She closed her eyes again, this time forever.

The hunters had fallen back, clutching each other and trembling like frightened rabbits. They weren't swaggering and bragging now.

Suddenly Mr. Povich found his tongue.

"She was a wolf woman!" he screeched. "A witch, living among us all this time, spreading her evil!"

Papa, who'd been swaying and shaking uncontrollably, made a moaning, choking sound and pitched forward on his face.

I was powerless to move. I just kept looking at Mama. And only one thought filled my mind. It filled my mind and my heart and my body until I thought I would die from the ache of it:

Mama was dead, and I hadn't told her how much I loved her.

THIRTEEN

·The·Next·Day·

We buried Mama the next morning—Papa, Pinky, and I—at the crossroads, out beyond Mrs. Kopek's farm.

Pinky said this is what we should do—that Mama would rest quietly here. Every spring, he said, when the wildflowers bloomed, strangers passing through would stop and wonder who was buried here and maybe say a prayer before they traveled on.

I didn't hate Pinky anymore. I knew now why he did what he did. And hadn't Mama called him her true friend and told him he did the right thing?

Joey kept asking what had happened to Mama.

"She went to heaven last night," Papa told him. "Mama is with the angels now."

Papa didn't say much else. He was white and tense, and the muscle in his jaw kept twitching and twitching.

When we came back from burying Mama, Papa went up into the attic and dragged down some suitcases and a trunk.

"What are you doing, Papa?" Joey asked. Poor little Joey. He had no idea what was going on around him. He kept clinging to me.

"We're leaving, Joey," Papa said. "We're going far away."

"But where are we going? Will Mama know how to find us?"

"Mama can find us anywhere now," Papa told him.

Papa moved slowly but steadily through the house, putting things into the trunk and suitcases that we would need in our new home: the good china, some pots and pans, our best clothes.

Then he called Pinky into the parlor and said, "I'm leaving everything to you. The house. The livestock. Everything."

"I don't want it," Pinky said. "I want nothing."

"I'm sure you don't. But take it anyway, Pinky. Sell it. Take the money and leave this accursed place and find yourself a home somewhere else."

"I'll send you the money, if you'll only give me an address," Pinky said.

"I don't want the money!" Papa was half shouting. "Don't you see? I want nothing to remind me of the years I've spent here."

Then Papa sat down at the desk, Mama's little desk, and wrote something on a long sheet of yellow paper.

"There. This ought to make it legal. I've deeded everything over to you, Pinky."

Pinky looked down at the paper and asked, "Does this mean I will never see you again?"

"Isn't it better that we never see each other again?" Papa said quietly.

Pinky bowed his head. "Yes. Yes, it would be better."

Papa seemed to be waiting for something all afternoon. Finally, at twilight, it came.

It was Mr. Povich. He arrived, as he had so many times, with all our neighbors behind him.

He didn't bang on the door this time. He just stood in the yard and shouted for Papa.

Before Papa opened the door, he told Pinky, "Go to the parlor and don't come out."

"Why? I want to stand beside you and show them I'm your friend."

"No! Stay out of it, Pinky. I want one of us, at least, to come out of this thing unbroken."

"That's impossible," Pinky said. "We're already broken. So let me prove my loyalty to you now, out there in front of those people."

"You can best prove your loyalty by making all my years here, fighting the winds and droughts, worthy of the effort," Papa said. "Can't you see, Pinky, that if you stay and sell my homestead, it will make everything I've done mean something?"

"I can still do that," Pinky argued.

"No. No you can't. All that bunch out there needs is an excuse to burn this place down. They'll do it for sure if you let them know you've been sympathetic to everything that happened with my wife."

Mr. Povich shouted again. "Are you coming out or do we have to go in there and drag you out?"

"Please, Pinky." Papa looked desperate. "Do it for me. Stay clear of this mess."

Pinky nodded reluctantly. He stepped forward, and he and Papa stood looking at each other. Then they awkwardly embraced. There was a feeling of finality in that embrace that even I, young as I was, recognized.

Pinky turned and kissed me, his hands caressing my hair, blessing me. He did the same to Joey. Then he turned and went into the parlor. The door closed on him, and that was the last I ever saw of Pinky.

Papa took a deep breath, opened the back door, and stepped out into the yard.

I stood in the doorway and watched. Joey came

over silently and leaned against me. I could feel him trembling, and I put my arms around him, pressing him close to my side so he couldn't see the hostile, menacing looks of the faces in the crowd, and the way they stared at us, all three of us, as if we were freaks.

Our neighbors stood ringed around Mr. Povich like hens around a banty rooster. Darkness was coming on fast, so most of them carried torches, just as they had that night when the hunters came to tell us how Mr. Findley had wounded . . . the white wolf.

Already I'd discovered it was easier if I made myself think of the white wolf as something separate from Mama.

"We want you out of this town!" Mr. Povich announced. "You and your filthy family. Now! Tonight!"

"I've been expecting you," Papa said evenly. "I thought you'd come earlier, but I see you preferred to wait until nightfall. It's more frightening this way, isn't it, in the dark and with torches?"

"There's a train arriving at the junction in an

hour," said Mr. Povich, undeterred. "If you leave now, we can get you there just in time. We want you and your demon offspring on it."

"Demon offspring? What are you talking about? My children have nothing to do with this!"

"Oh yeah? With an animal for a mother? They're wolf seed. Witch's brats. Lice breed nits, you know, and we don't want them around here, mixing with decent people."

"All right, Mr. Povich," Papa replied. "We'll leave. But for my reasons, not yours. I'm already packed. If you'll just give us a few minutes to collect our coats and bags, we'll be right with you."

They loaded our trunk and suitcases on Mr. Povich's sleigh, and we set out for the train station.

It was a short trip, but somewhere along the way, my childhood slipped from me, and I became an eternity older.

The train waited at the station, puffing and throbbing.

The whole town seemed to be there.

I looked around at the people I'd known all my life.

Their faces were almost unrecognizable, twisted as they were with fear and hate and anger, the flickering of the torches heightening the ugliness and the evil.

The train panted like a wolf.

A wounded wolf . . .

▪ Chicago—1910 ▪

But how could it be?" I ask Papa. "Mama. A wolf.
Mama, turning herself into a wolf."

I know the answer, but still I wait for it.

We rarely speak about what happened in Canada, Papa and I. We rarely mention Mama. At
least not in front of Joey. We want him to forget
her. Joey doesn't know about Mama being a . . .
what she was. He only knows that she died suddenly four years ago, under mysterious circumstances. Papa and I want to keep it that way for
him.

As for Papa and me, what happened to Mama was so terrible, so unspeakable, that neither of us can bear to talk about it.

But now my nightmares have begun. We must talk about it.

It's nearly dawn. Rosy ribbons of light, faint and flushed, are beginning to creep upward, past the rooftops, pushing back the night.

My nightmare tonight roused both of us. Papa heard me cry out through the wall that separates our bedrooms. We are sitting on the sofa in the living room now. Joey is asleep. Safe.

Papa has lit a fire in the fireplace to take away the early-morning chill. He holds my hands tightly in his, the way he always does when we talk.

He looks old and frail, as if his strength and vigor have been sucked from him.

"Mama was a wolf woman," I repeat.

"Yes," Papa says. "It sounds like one of Pinky's old Russian folktales, doesn't it? But it happened. Maybe that's what folktales are—remembrances of things that have really happened."

I remove my hands gently from his and press them to my temples. "It's hard to think of Mama as an animal. A monster."

"Your mama was half human and half wolf, Therese, not a monster. I don't know how it came to be. Perhaps, someday, some scientist will be able to explain how things like this happen."

"But, Papa—"

"Mama was kind and pure and good. Most animals are, you know. It's humans who do terrible things to each other. There are no monster animals, Therese, only monster people."

He shifts a little on the sofa. "That's what you should always remember about Mama," Papa says. "Remember only the love. And we did have a lot of love, didn't we?"

"But how can I continue to live with what happened?" I ask. "How have you lived with it, Papa?"

Papa gets up stiffly and goes over to the fireplace. He picks up the poker and jabs halfheartedly at the log fire.

"Terrible things happen to people, Therese.

Things that shouldn't happen to us. Things we don't deserve. Yet we survive. We keep on going. Down through the centuries it has been this way. It will always be this way."

As if in response to his words, a splinter of a burning log sparks, and little glowing bits flutter up toward the chimney and then fall down again, dead and blackened, breaking into a thousand powdery pieces.

Just like Mama, I think, looking at them. A brief, beautiful, bright blaze, and then . . . ashes. Cold, dead ashes.

"But my nightmares, Papa—"

"You're getting older, Therese. More emotional. More imaginative. And this has invaded your dreams. Things will settle down in time. Meanwhile, though, you must be strong. You must tell yourself that everything passes. That you will survive everything that has happened to you."

Then, fearfully, I bring up the thing that worries me most. The thing I've put off asking Papa.

"Do you remember what Mr. Povich said? About Joey and me being wolf seed? Do you think we will ever . . . ? I mean, she was our mother, and maybe we will be what she was."

Papa crosses the floor in two strides. He sits down beside me, takes my arm, and grips it so tightly I wince in pain.

"No! I won't let it happen, Therese! You and Joey look like me, not your mother. You resemble me. You have my body, even down to the way your fingernails grow. If you have inherited my body, then it will never turn into that of a . . ."

"A wolf, Papa?" I ask quietly. "I hope not. But if it should?"

"It won't," Papa said. "My love was not enough to save your mother. It was already too late when I first saw her. But you are mine! I've loved both you and Joey from the moment you were born. I will surround you with love. I will make a fortress of my love. If I do that, nothing can ever harm you."

"Yes, Papa."

I look at him, but not the way a child usually looks at its father, fond and unseeing. I'm looking deep into Papa's eyes.

His eyes are hooded and withdrawn, as if he is gazing into the future and wondering what it holds. . . .

And so, to save him further pain, I do not tell him about tonight's dream. That it differed slightly, but frighteningly so, from the others:

Again, I dreamed of flaring torches and glittering snow and the sound of people shouting. And the train, and the terrible animal sound it makes.

And again, I dreamed of Mama in her long white gown splashed with blood all down the front. Her arms were stretched out to me.

But in this dream, those outstretched arms were not an appeal for help. They were trying to protect me from something. Danger. An approaching danger, I think. Her pale lips called a warning I could not hear.

And then I heard the howling of the wolves, the ones that in my dreams are always calling to Mama.

Only now, this time, they were calling to me.